The Poison People

He rolled fast to his left, out of bed, to the floor. A bullet thumped into the bedhead above him. Simultaneously there was another shot. This one was outside the room. The head at the window had disappeared.

He crawled towards the window cautiously, then even more cautiously raised his head. There was more light in the compound now, lamps and men. Two were loading a third on a canvas stretcher, another standing guard above them. Russell could see his rifle clearly. It was modern with a modern night sight. The little party of four, three living, one dead, began to move away at a trot. They moved towards a decaying hedge, disappearing through a convenient gap. Charles Russell's hearing was still acute and he heard what he thought were van doors opening, the noise of the stretcher sliding in. Then the doors as they shut and the engine starting. For a moment they revved it, then noise faded away.

... That was very slick work, very neat indeed.

Other titles in the Walker British Mystery series:

Marian Babson • THE LORD MAYOR OF DEATH
John Creasey • HELP FROM THE BARON
Elizabeth Lemarchand • UNHAPPY RETURNS
W.J. Burley • DEATH IN WILLOW PATTERN
John Sladek • INVISIBLE GREEN
William Haggard • YESTERDAY'S ENEMY
Elizabeth Lemarchand • STEP IN THE DARK
Simon Harvester • ZION ROAD
Peter Alding • MURDER IS SUSPECTED
John Creasey • THE TOFF AND THE FALLEN ANGELS
J.G. Jeffreys • SUICIDE MOST FOUL
Simon Harvester • MOSCOW ROAD
Josephine Bell • VICTIM
John Creasey • THE BARON AND THE UNFINISHED PORTRAIT
Jeffrey Ashford • THREE LAYERS OF GUILT
Elizabeth Lemarchand • CHANGE FOR THE WORSE
Marian Babson • DANGEROUS TO KNOW
William Haggard • VISA TO LIMBO
Desmond Cory • THE NIGHT HAWK
Jeffrey Ashford • SLOW DOWN THE WORLD

WILLIAM HAGGARD
Poison People

WALKER AND COMPANY · NEW YORK

Copyright © William Haggard 1977

All rights reserved. No part of this book may be reproduced or transmitted in any form or by any means, electric or mechanical, including photocopying, recording, or by any information storage and retrieval system, without permission in writing from the Publisher.

All the characters and events portrayed in this story are fictitious.

First published in the United States of America in 1979 by the Walker Publishing Company, Inc.

This paperback edition first published in 1983.

ISBN: 0-8027-3031-0

Library of Congress Catalog Card Number: 78-68540

Printed in the United States of America

10 9 8 7 6 5 4 3 2 1

ONE

1

Colonel Charles Russell, lately of the Security Executive, was walking to his flat after lunch. He was normally equable, often quite happy, for he had trained himself never to worry or fuss. If he hadn't, his work would have killed him years ago, the double burden of running the Security Executive. On one shoulder had sat what he saw as his duty, on the other the knowledge of total loneliness, the certainty that if something went wrong his political masters would promptly disown him. Some high principled ass would stand up in the House, or more likely a man of the far, far Left, and if he could make his assertion half stick Charles Russell would be dismissed in disgrace. He might even find himself in prison, for though he'd bent the law he was never beyond it.

His present problem was slight in proportion. He shook his shoulders—this wouldn't do. A lifetime's discipline returned reassuringly. He wasn't going to live for ever, and meanwhile he had good health and friends, he was a man in modestly comfortable circumstances. It sounded better in Latin. *Carpe diem*.

He permitted a smile: there was something else. To a vigorous man in late middle age, the greatest enemy was always boredom and Charles Russell was very seldom bored.

But however effective his private discipline he couldn't escape the misfortunes of others. They moved him as his own troubles did not, for beneath his urbane and detached exterior was an Anglo-Irishman's ready sympathy. Poor Willy, he thought, poor Willy Fenwick. It had all gone wrong for him cruelly and bitterly.

He had just been giving Charles Russell lunch, and the meal itself had, as always, been good. The food, then, had been excellent, but nothing else had been even tolerable. For Willy Fenwick was a very old friend and Fenwick had seemed near to defeat. The bottom had fallen out of his world and Russell thought him too old to start building another.

No, but he might pull one down if he could find who had really killed his son; not the dope pedlars but the man behind them.

In a different age and social climate there'd been a pejorative word for the William Fenwicks who'd made their own fortunes and earned their honours. His ambition had been to Found a Family. Charles Russell considered that somewhat old-fashioned, but he also considered it understandable. Superior persons might smile in their sleeves, call it vulgar and even anti-social, but if that had been Willy Fenwick's ambition, Charles Russell, though he didn't share it, could see nothing disgraceful and much that was praiseworthy.

And now this ambition had fallen in dust. Willy Fenwick had had a single son, by a wife who had made his life a misery, and this son had just died in a London nursing home. A discreet and rather unusual nursing home since the son had been a hopeless junkie. Charles Russell had known this for months—so had Willy. But the actual death had hit Fenwick hard. The last weeks had put ten years on his age; he was now obsessed with the lust for revenge. Some people would have called him mad and there were pseudoscientific words for it all. Charles Russell used neither, mistrusting both. He had never had a son himself, or none whom he had wished to acknowledge, but he could understand that Sir William Fenwick, for the time at least, was distinctly unbalanced.

Russell increased his pace without knowing it, unconsciously trying to escape from reflection. He went round a corner and almost fell. The cat which had almost tripped him mewed.

Charles Russell recovered his balance and swore. But not at the cat: he swore at his clumsiness. To the cat he said: 'Good afternoon, cat.' He liked animals but was unsentimental, so he spoke to the cat in his ordinary voice, not the special tone people used to beasts. He didn't believe the old wives' tale that they understood every word you said to them, but it was tiresome and even condescending to talk down to a cat or a dog or a baby.

He said to the cat: 'May I suggest you watch your front? If you'd had me down I'd have broken a leg.'

The cat didn't answer but she'd taken to Russell. She came up and waved her tail politely, then she rubbed against Charles Russell's legs. He bent down and as he stroked her she moved away. Charles Russell followed.

It was only a foot but it saved his life. The cat saw the falling body first and jumped with a feline scream of outrage. Charles Russell didn't see it at all. Something came past his head as a blur. There was a sickening crunch on the asphalt pavement.

Russell jumped too, not as fast as the cat, straightening his back as he did so. The body was on the pavement motionless. The head was face up but was split like an apple.

Charles Russell had seen many deaths so he did not need to feel for a pulse. The face was intact, still frozen in terror. The rest of the head was not. He looked away.

But not before a clear recognition. He knew this man, for he'd once employed him. He'd been a high-class safebreaker but was now living honestly. Harry Maxim, that was, on the bitter pavement. Harry Maxim with face unmarked. The rest. . . .

People had collected from nowhere, as people in London always did. It was the same on some uninhabited moor: one moment there wasn't a soul in sight and the next, on some provoking incident, there was a considerable and increasing crowd. Russell picked on a middle-aged woman deliberately. She wore sturdy shoes and she wasn't chattering.

'There's a telephone round the corner, madam.' He knew these quiet streets as he knew his hand. 'Go round it and turn right. On your left. Ring Nine-Nine-Nine for the police and an ambulance.'

She looked at him and finally nodded. Authority she had known and could recognize. She hadn't been sick and she hadn't nattered.

Charles Russell looked at the house above him. Flats it would be and rather expensive ones. Five floors above was a splintered window frame.

. . . He must have jumped in a panic or maybe been thrown.

Russell walked up the steps to the open front door and in the hall he read the name-cards reflectively. Two of them were clearly foreign but one of these lived on the bottom floor and Maxim's head would not be pulp if he'd fallen only a matter of feet. The other was Indian, V. S. Sen, and this other was on the fifth floor. Russell thought.

It wasn't an uncommon name but to Charles Russell it was also informative. Almost certainly some sort of Bengali. Charles Russell had seen service in India but had escaped the two traps which that country baited. One was the trap of contempt, the other of love. He had escaped still sane, or liked to think so, but he'd returned without the smallest illusion. He rang the bell beside the nameplate. At first nothing happened; he rang again. The speaker beside the nameplate crackled. 'Yes,' it said. 'What is it, please?'

The esses were very faintly sibilant, not the lilt of the Eurasian half-caste, but the speech of the university Indian who would often speak English at home for practice.

'There's been an accident in the street outside.'

'I fear I cannot help you, sir.'

'That may well be the case but I think you should try. A man has fallen out of this building. The man is dead but I've called a doctor.'

'I assure you, sir . . .'

'And also the police. I see you have a window in matchwood. If you do not come down then the police will come up. Which they'll probably wish to do in any case.'

A silence and some talk in the background. The voice said at last:

'I'm a diplomat. I shall claim my privileges.'

'Just as you please.'

'Even so, I shall come.'

Charles Russell went back to the street in silence, wiping his mind of too easy impressions. The knot of people had swollen magically. Two women were weeping, most men had their hats off. The wail of a police car's siren was moving closer. Russell judged it at three streets away.

He stood and watched the door of the flats, surprised when he saw three men come out of it. One, he was sure, would be V. S. Sen, stoutish and very clearly nervous, but the other two were turbaned Sikhs, and Sikhs despised Bengalis heartily. They were the protestants of the Hindu octopus and monotheists at least in theory, a race which had escaped the labyrinth of the countless forms of the never defined. They were also — perhaps more relevant now — a people who did the solid work. You found them as foremen, drivers, policemen. They also made excellent private guards. Russell looked at the pair with increasing interest. They had the typically stocky legs, the powerful shoulders, the air of competence. They might not have a Bengali's brains but they would do what no Bengali would dare to.

Such as throwing a man through a window to his death. Russell didn't love Sikhs but was prepared to respect them.

He walked up to them as the three men came out. 'I'm the man who rang your bell. My name is Russell.'

The man who was Sen said: 'Where is the accident?'

The police car had arrived by now and the crowd had thinned to make way for its occupants. The body was visible through the gap. So was the stain on the pavement. It had spread.

For a moment Charles Russell thought Sen would vomit but he controlled himself and turned away. He was moaning softly and shivering violently, then he put up his hands to hide his eyes. It was an effeminate gesture and Russell noticed it. He was learning something of V. S. Sen; nothing of the two Sikhs but what he knew. When the hands came down Russell looked at the face. One of two slightly protruding teeth, the canines in the upper jaw, had been caught outside the lower lip. Russell had seen this often before.

A policeman was clearing the knot of bystanders, taking names and making way for the ambulance. A second, a sergeant, came up to Russell who had noticed him look up at the window. The sergeant had seen it was broken, not open. He pointed at it and spoke to Russell.

'You're the owner of that flat, sir?'

'No. I'm the man who asked a woman to ring you.'

'You saw the accident?'

'Not exactly. I live near here and was walking home. A falling body narrowly missed me.'

'Then your name and address, please.'

Russell gave them. To his astonishment the sergeant saluted. 'An honour sir,' he said.

'You know me?' Charles Russell had not supposed he would. He'd been retired for several years and was modest.

The sergeant said with a hint of asperity: 'If it isn't an impertinence, sir, perhaps you've been watching too much telly. The police drive about like dummies in motor cars—you'd think we did nothing else for our money. But we do know our patches too, we really do. If there's anyone of consequence living there it's a very poor policeman who doesn't know it.'

'I beg your pardon.'

'Not at all.' The sergeant turned to face the three Indians. 'Gentlemen?'

A second of silence.

'Does one of you gentlemen own that flat?'

Sen said: 'I do. The flat is mine. But I'm an Attaché to my High Commission.'

'And these other two?'

'The Commission's servants.' The tooth on the lower lip had disappeared.

The sergeant opened his mouth to speak but shut it as Russell broke in urbanely. 'When I was working I met this difficulty. A diplomat has unquestioned privileges but also he has obligations. Not to obstruct the police, for instance, in an inquiry into a simple accident.'

'An accident,' Sen said. 'Yes, of course. You wish to inspect my flat, then?'

'Please.'

'I must telephone my superiors.'

'Certainly.'

The ambulance men had removed the body by the time the Attaché returned to the pavement. 'I have had my instructions. Please come in.'

The sergeant turned to Russell politely. 'May I ask you to come as well?'

'Whatever for?'

'An independent witness is always useful. Moreover you know more of immunity than I do or am ever likely to. If I make the smallest mistake please check me.'

'I doubt if I'll have to.' Russell said. It was his opinion, though he didn't offer it, that this sergeant would not stay a sergeant for long.

They went up in the lift and Sen opened the door. The living room was a total shambles, chairs and tables broken, ornaments smashed. In one corner was a modern safe and the room held a very faint smell of explosives. The door of the safe was ajar, the safe empty. Russell saw one Sikh look at the other. Sen pointed at the safe and said:

'We found him just as he'd managed to open it.'

'I see,' the sergeant said. 'I see.'

'He resisted apprehension stoutly.' The sentence was correct enough but to Russell it was also interesting. It told him that Sen was scared again, he was slipping into babu English.

'I see,' the sergeant said once more. He considered, then looked at the Sikhs standing silently. 'These men, er, tried to apprehend him?'

'Oh yes, that is so. That is so indeed.' The sibilants hissed like angry snakes. 'There was terrible fight, oh dreadful conflict.' The English was slipping badly now, the articles slurred and indeed elided.

He's lying, Russell thought. But why?

'Who are these men?'

'They guard the Commission.'

'Then why are they here?'

'To protect my work.' Sen began to explain, too fast and too fluently; he pointed at the safe dramatically. 'That safe held my code books, you see. They are secret. When I use them I must always be guarded.'

The sergeant looked at Russell but neither spoke.

'So if I've got this right it goes something like this. You returned to your flat to do some coding. With code books which I assume you've removed. You brought these guards as your rules required. On entry you found an unknown man who had tampered with your safe. Correct?'

'Oh yes indeed. Correct. Quite right.'

'Was there anything else in that safe but your code books?'

'Nothing at all. I assure you, sir. Nothing.'

'It's a pretty big safe just to keep your code books.'

'It is the one they sent to my flat for the purpose. The administration man, I mean.'

'Let's leave that for the moment, then. When you found this man breaking your safe did you challenge him?'

'I beg your pardon?'

'Did you ask him what he was doing?'

'Of course. But he did not answer. He flew against us.'

'What happened then?'

'I told you. There was a shocking struggle.'

'The results of which I can see for myself.' The sergeant's voice went down two tones. 'But not how the man fell out of your window.'

'I did not see. I am not man of violence.'

'You mean you didn't join in the fighting? Then the better reason to see what happened.'

'I cannot be sure. I am now all confounded. They were fighting all over the room, it was terrible. Near the window they were all three together, wrestling and hitting. I think he tripped. There was a crash and he was gone in an instant.' Sen was now weeping a trifle too noisily.

'Can your friends speak English?'

'Only a little.'

'Then I'll arrange for an interpreter later. For the moment I needn't trouble you further.' The sergeant turned to Russell. 'Nor you, sir. And thank you.'

Charles Russell walked back to his flat reflectively. The matter was certainly none of his business, but more than one detail had struck him as curious. He was sure that V. S. Sen had lied, for his English had slipped from a slick cool competence to the jargon of a frightened student. There might well be an explanation of that since few men of his race could stand much pressure, but why had Harry Maxim been there? Charles Russell hadn't told the police that he'd recognized the man in the street, far less that he had once employed him. They'd find out his ordinary criminal record which would corroborate the Indian's story. Up to a point, that is, but not beyond. So a man with a serious criminal record, but one who'd been going straight, had relapsed. He'd gone to a diplomat's flat to steal from it. . . .

Charles Russell was disinclined to believe it. He'd kept in touch with Harry Maxim's affairs, as he kept in touch with most who had served him. He had married a girl with a private income and they lived in a comfortable flat in Weybridge. Harry himself worked with metal somewhere.

Charles Russell smiled. He'd be exceptionally good at it.

And even supposing the man had reverted, he wasn't the

sort to fall through a window. He could look after himself, he'd been tough and resourceful. But a couple of Sikh strongarms . . . Hm.

Russell let himself in and mixed a drink. It was futile to worry, these things had a pattern. Either they dropped dead at your feet or else they began to develop interestingly. He'd be called to the inquest of course, and he'd say his piece. Not that he could tell them much, but the little he knew he'd recite on oath. They'd hardly ask him if he'd known Maxim—why should they? So he'd say his piece and that would end it. Reason said loudly that that would end it but an instinct behind it whispered insidiously.

This was going to be another involvement, there'd be developments if he wasn't mistaken.

Which were now taking place in Sen's wrecked living room. He was reporting to his second master, who wasn't the Republic of India, and certainly not its current ruler whom he and most Indians called the Presence. The Presence stood for orthodox politics, as unchanging as the country itself, the wheeler-dealing and the power of patronage, above all for the Byzantine corruption, its tendrils as strong as poison ivy, from the sham splendours of the country's capital to the post office of the meanest village. But this other man's power was wealth, great wealth, for he and only a handful of others were all that the Presence had left unbroken of what had once been the country's powerful plutocracy. He was a Marwadi—money was in his blood. His empire had come under harsh attack but if its wings had been clipped it had not yet been broken. The Presence would happily see him dead, but he wasn't yet dead, he was active and cunning. He'd trade in anything that showed a profit and that anything included heroin.

He read Sen's report again and frowned. That Russell could be extremely dangerous.

2

Russell had bathed and shaved next morning and was eating a cooked breakfast contentedly when there was a ring at the door. His housekeeper answered it. He heard voices, one a man's, one hers, then her clear Highland lisp. 'Please wait while I ask him.'

She returned and stood before Russell's table. She was tall and spare and spoke Gaelic with friends, and she'd been serving Charles Russell for eighteen years. She stood erect, hands folded before her.

'He says he's an Inspector of Police.'

'Is he in uniform?'

'No, he is not.'

'Did you ask to see his warrant?'

'Should I?' No Highlander gave an inch unnecessarily.

Charles Russell laughed. 'Does he look like a policeman? You know what I mean.'

'No, I don't think he looks like a policeman particularly.' She had the Scotswoman's punctilious mind. 'Just the same I'd risk a shilling he is one.'

'I bow to your instinct. Please send him in.'

The man she showed in was powerfully built, perhaps in his middle thirties, collected. Russell asked him to sit but he didn't immediately.

'I owe you an explanation, sir, since I couldn't help hearing what your housekeeper said to you. But I don't claim to be an Inspector of Police, only to have been one once. Lesley King, at your service.'

'Sit down just the same.'

The visitor did so and Russell considered him. His shoes were good and beautifully kept—Russell always looked at a man's shoes first—his clothes were formal, his tie subdued, and he had an air of solid professional sobriety. Russell knew all about ex-Inspectors. Mostly they had left in a hurry, and if the scandal hadn't been too overt they found jobs in some private detective agency. But somehow he doubted if King had done that.

Apparently King had read his thoughts for he held up a hand and smiled a denial. He was courteous but faintly ironical. 'No, sir, I don't work for an agency. I am working for a single man.'

'May I ask for whom?'

'Sir William Fenwick.'

'Are you indeed.'

'You would like me to prove it? That's perfectly reasonable.' Again there was the faint note of irony. 'If you care to ring him he'll confirm what I say.'

'How do you know I even know him?'

'I know a good deal more than that. I know that you had lunch with him yesterday and that he told you of the death of his son. He also explained how that death occurred. He told me these things himself.'

'I see.' Charles Russell decided this man was genuine. They had lunched at Fenwick's house alone. 'And Sir William sent you here to see me?'

'No, sir, I came of my own accord—the accident which you witnessed yesterday.'

'How do you know about that?'

'I didn't resign from the police under any cloud. I have friends in it still, besides other contacts.'

'Does that accident affect Sir William?'

'Not directly but it affects the timing.'

'Timing of what?'

'Sir William's intention. He has hired me to smash a drug ring finally, the one which drove his son to his death.'

'Laudable,' Russell said, 'but dangerous. Any particular qualifications?'

'Only that I was once in the Drug Squad.'

Russell had already guessed it, for there was something about this cool young man which was over and above a routine police background. He had noticed it before in specialists, an almost religious dedication. He considered Lesley King again, the polite assured manner, the faint ring of irony. He was impressed by him, was prepared to like him, but he wouldn't trust Lesley King a yard if they were standing on different sides of a fence, the frail fence of what was called right and wrong.

To hell with that—who was he to pass judgement? King had said he'd left the police with honour and Charles Russell was inclined to believe him. They hadn't threatened dismissal or even hinted, but drugs were a hideous, shameful trade, the law's weapons to fight it a criminal jest. The pushers were fairly easy to net but the big men had all the protection they needed. So something was slipped in a big man's pocket. . . .

Of course he would claim he'd been planted—routine. Happily it was so much routine that juries had begun to discount it.

Happily? He had thought of 'happily'? Then again, who was he to pass judgement? He had bent the law double himself and done it cheerfully. Life wasn't a choice between good and evil, it was a choice between great wrongs and lesser. He looked at Lesley King again, respect warming into a sense of community. They had one thing in common and that was important. Both had been unashamedly dedicated. Russell thought Fenwick had chosen wisely.

He returned from reflection to Lesley King. 'We were discussing an unfortunate accident.'

'If it was an accident.'

'Wasn't it?'

'No.'

Russell almost asked: 'How do you know?' but didn't. This was going too fast, he must slow it down. 'The Indian who owned the flat told a story which I thought was strange. He said that his safe held official code books and that he had to have guards when he took them out. That was why the two Sikhs were with him. You know about them?'

King nodded briefly. 'Then do you believe Mr. Sen's story?'

'Even Indians wouldn't let ciphers outside an embassy.'

'Then the man who broke in wasn't after code books? Code books which you've agreed weren't there.'

'Have I agreed to that? In terms?'

'Colonel, stop playing.' King was polite still, but suddenly formidable. Charles Russell didn't resent the comment. He was prepared to play it straight and happy to do so. He said in his urbanest manner:

'Since you've come to me I'm assuming a purpose. Presumably that's advice or help, but if I'm going to give you either you'll have to put the cards on the table.'

'I had hoped you'd say that. I'm very grateful.' King paused to collect his thoughts, then went on. 'The man who broke into Sen's flat was financed by myself with Sir William's money. He was an ex-peterman who was going straight. I had to pay him a pretty large sum.'

'His name was Harry Maxim, I think.'

For the first time Lesley King showed surprise. 'That hasn't been in the papers yet.'

'It doesn't have to be in the papers. I knew him since I'd used him myself.' Russell added without a muscle moving: 'You'll realize that the Security Executive wasn't run like a middle-class kindergarten. Nor, I rather suspect, is the Drug Squad. But I hadn't seen Harry Maxim for years. I'd heard he had married a girl with some money and was going straight in a comfortable job. We always tried to keep in touch and sometimes we could repay a service. But Maxim didn't need help till yesterday and then it was much too late to give it. But I recognized his face at once.'

'Did you tell this to the police?'

'Why should I?'

Ex-Inspector King laughed softly. 'Your reputation does not belie you, sir. And now its my turn to lay one down.'

'It had better be a good one.'

'It is. It wasn't code books in that safe. It was heroin.'

'You're sure? The stuff which killed Fenwick's son?'

'It was.'

'It's beginning to make sense,' Russell said.

'I told you I was once in the Drug Squad and I haven't been wasting Sir William's money. Have you been to Leicester recently?'

'Not for some years.'

'It's changed remarkably. Parts of it are wholly Indian—they even have their own public houses. It cost a good deal of Fenwick's money but in time I got the name of the Big Boy. He's in India but he comes here often.'

'Steady,' Russell said. 'Go steady.'

'We shall have to go steady till our number comes up. But those Indians are still flogging heroin. A Messenger brings it in in his Bag and Sen's flat is the major cache where they hide it. It's distributed from there to the Midlands and I sent Maxim in to get the proof. The Sikhs weren't present to guard any code books. They were there to collect the drug and run it out. When they saw the safe open they whipped all the drug out—it was probably on their persons still when you and that sergeant went up to the flat—but thereafter they lost their heads completely. Perhaps Maxim fought hard to get away but in any case they wouldn't have let him. He had seen what could blow the whole ring sky high. He didn't fall from that window. They pushed him through it.'

Charles Russell rang the bell for coffee. He thought fast but he needed a minimum time. Over the shared coffee he said:

'You talked about their losing their heads.'

King nodded.

'Perhaps you're right, they often do. But if they did they have also been lucky.'

'Which I rather think is more than you have.' Lesley King was very polite but decided.

'Tell me why,' Russell said.

'Big Boy is more than big enough to have learnt that his stuff killed Fenwick's son, Fenwick who's rich and known to be tough. So if a man was found searching that Indian's flat it's going to be a pretty fair bet that he was doing so on behalf of Fenwick. And who was outside standing watch?

Colonel Russell.'

'Coincidence. I live almost next door.'

'And are also an old friend of Fenwick's.'

Russell thought it over carefully; finally he said quietly: 'I see.'

'Big Boy's pretty big.'

'I believe you. And thank you for the delicate warning.'

'Then may I ask you what you're going to say at the inquest?'

'I shall say what I must say and nothing more, a good citizen doing his public duty. Nothing about Maxim's work for me. I shall say that a falling body narrowly missed me and that later the police took me up to the flat. I shan't comment on that unless anyone else does and I doubt if they will since the action was sensible. Sen had talked about his special status, he had even demanded to ring his bosses, so it was wise to have a neutral observer. That sergeant should be commended.'

'He has been.'

'Then what I saw upstairs fits neatly with the hypothesis of an ordinary safe-breaking.' Charles Russell stiffened, his manner changing. The urbanity had gone with the wind and a cool authority taken its place. 'But why should any statement I make be of interest to an ex-Inspector? Or for that matter to Sir William Fenwick?'

'We don't want the gun to go off at half cock. We want the whole network smashed to pieces and we haven't had time to plan in detail. So we want it to look what they'll say it was, what you yourself called an ordinary safe-breaking.'

'Won't the police be suspicious?'

'I *know* they're suspicious, but the police are also hamstrung helplessly. This is politics, Colonel Russell—the Commonwealth. The public might praise them for breaking this ring but there'd be officials who'd be much embarrassed, who'd do everything short of murder to cover up. Sir William is a politician and he knows that even better than I do. That's why he hired me. May I say I went gladly.'

'A happy worker is mostly a good one.'

'Was that a reproof?'

'Very far from it — a recommendation. I suspect my old friend Willie Fenwick is temporarily a little dotty.'

'I'm perfectly sure he's a little dotty. That suits me fine — I'm dotty too. On the matter of dealing in drugs, that is.'

Charles Russell let it go without comment. 'Shall I see you at the inquest?'

'You will not.'

When King had gone Russell lit a cigar. He shared King's hatred of all traffic in drugs and when it was being run by a diplomat. . . .

Diplomats — he had always shunned them. They pompously scurried to and fro while the real work was done by faceless men whose names you would seldom see in the papers. But they had privileges and absurdly great ones. The *chers collègues* would always stick together since a great scandal wouldn't suit their books. Russell put his cigar aside; he wasn't feeling like smoking, he felt slightly sick.

Two days later he attended the inquest and it had been exactly as he had supposed it would be. The bored and dingy Coroner, a man who had failed in his own profession, hadn't exactly raced the proceedings, but if his golf clubs hadn't been physically visible their existence had always been present in spirit. He had called Charles Russell who had given his evidence. He'd been walking along the street to his flat when a body had fallen and narrowly missed him. Looking up he had seen a broken window. He'd been fairly sure that the man had been dead, but just in case he still had life he had stayed with him and sent a bystander to telephone for the police and an ambulance. The former had arrived very promptly and when the owner of the broken window appeared and claimed diplomatic status the sergeant of police had asked Charles Russell to accompany him up to the flat. There he had seen the signs of a struggle, a safe and a safebreaker's tools beside it.

'Thank you, Colonel Russell. I'm much obliged.'

The Coroner had asked no questions and his jury had sat silent throughout. They were every bit as bored as he was. Other witnesses had corroborated, and Sen had told his story smoothly. Since there wasn't any question of punishment the police had disclosed what they knew of Maxim: the deceased had had a criminal record. The Coroner had looked at the jury who had clearly made up their minds already. They returned a unanimous verdict promptly but the Coroner had not quite finished. Looking at V. S. Sen too coyly he contrived a rather greasy sentence about regretting the inconvenience, nay outrage, to the person of an honoured guest from a country with such close ties with his own .

They all got up and went home or to offices. It was finished, tied up. The case was closed.

But to Russell it wasn't and that by an accident. For the following day he'd been reading the paper at breakfast and, as always, he'd looked at the Births and Deaths. Many men of his age had the same dour habit but in Russell's there was nothing of malice. It gave him no pleasure that friends and contemporaries hadn't shared in his own remarkable vigour; he read solely to inform himself, since he was a punctilious man and conscious of duty. It wouldn't do if some friend of ancient standing were buried without so much as a wreath from him.

Particularly if that friend were a woman. When they met again, if they ever did, he could hardly expect an affectionate welcome.

So he looked at the notice of Maxim's funeral with something more than a casual interest. It was true that he'd hardly been a friend but he'd worked successfully for the Executive twice, and one of those times had been very important. Russell stared out of the window uncertainly. It was raining in sheets and his golf had been cancelled. He was going to be rather bored that morning, and a funeral, if not precisely amusing, would at least pass the time till he lunched at his club. He hadn't time to send flowers so he'd go himself.

He went into his bedroom and changed; if you did a thing at all you did it properly. He changed his golf clothes to a formal suit, black tie and bowler hat, umbrella. Then he rang for a taxi to Waterloo where he bought a first class return to Weybridge. The carriage was littered and filthy as usual, a disgrace to any western country. At Weybridge he found another taxi, directing it to St. Saviour's church. He dismissed it and put the umbrella up, standing in the rain, slightly shivering. He'd passed the cortège on the way to the church for his driver had been young and impetuous. In the churchyard there was a small knot of figures but the principals hadn't yet arrived.

He went into the church and sighed. The outside had been sufficiently ugly but the inside, in Russell's opinion, was worse, high Victorian and graceless gothic, a snug shrine to the virtues of rich suburbia. Charles Russell preferred the round arch to the pointed, and this huge, half-decaying, soulless barn had lowered his spirits rudely another degree.

He gave the procession four minutes precisely, then went out into the grim, damp churchyard. The knot of mourners was indeed a small one, but Russell was not surprised at that. Criminals would take care of each other, they'd look after a woman while her man was in jail, but they weren't notably attached to funerals. Maxim had been going straight and had probably lost the friends of his trade. His others, if he'd made any, had stayed at home on this terrible day. . . . Four men who Russell thought were mutes, a priest and a tall woman in black. Russell bowed to her and the priest read the service. He didn't exactly gabble his way though it but his manner contrived to express his knowledge that this man had not led a blameless life. In any case he had richer parishioners.

When it was over Charles Russell bowed again, surprised when the woman walked up to him firmly. She held herself well and her black was elegant. Behind her veil was an oval face and very blue eyes below handsome eyebrows.

'Colonel Russell?' she asked.

He nodded, waiting.

'I guessed it might be. Thank you for coming. My husband sometimes spoke of you.' Behind the veil he could see a cool little smile. 'He was discreet of course, and so am I.'

'I'm very glad indeed of that.'

Charles Russell considered, watching the woman, for he'd have confessed to a very unusual uncertainty. She had the manner of an assured position and her speech was not that of Harry Maxim. If she saw his doubt she slipped his hook neatly.

'As you see, there won't be entertainment'—she looked at the priest and the mutes with contempt—'but you deserve a drink on a day like this. Shall we go to my flat?'

'That would be very nice.'

. . . . I'm a fool.

They climbed into her car, not a cheap one, and she drove fast and with an evident skill to a modern block of flats on the hill. She had raised her veil to drive the car. With it she had looked attractive, without it she was a good deal more.

She let him in and he looked around quietly. He was good at judging a background quickly and this wasn't what he'd expected to find. The car and the clothes had said adequate means and he'd expected the taste of superior Weybridge, but this living room was a street from that, shabby-elegant, comfortable, rather old-fashioned. There were some very good pieces, surely authentic, and in a corner a baby grand piano. Russell looked at it and suppressed a start. On the top was a single photograph, framed. It was a photograph of Sir William Fenwick.

She read his thoughts and laughed at him pleasantly. 'Not what you think at all. My father. And a very generous father he was and is.'

'I didn't know Willy had a daughter.'

'He hasn't, or not by the late Lady Fenwick. The late unlamented Lady Fenwick.' She handed him a gin and tonic. 'I know you know my father well. What did you think of his lady wife?'

'Not a fair question.'

'No, I suppose such a question isn't.' She was friendly but like her father determined. 'But you met her?'

'Once or twice at his house.'

'I met her too once or twice of course, but she would never consent to receive me formally. She was that sort of woman, you know.'

'I had heard so.'

'She married him for his money — no more. Then she played with him like a cat with a sparrow. She had a good deal to do with the state he's in now, and when my half-brother died the way he did, daddy went quietly round the bend.' She added with an unmistakable pride: 'My father still sees my mother regularly.'

She rose to mix another drink but he stopped her with an inhibiting hand. He needed to think and to think alone. He wasn't a man who could lie with conviction but social untruths he could manage fluently. He looked at his watch and smiled politely. 'I'm sorry that I've an engagement for lunch. I'll have to get back to London quickly.'

If Penny Maxim was surprised she hid it. 'Then I'll drive you to the station.'

'Very kind.'

In the car he made his mind up quickly. He still needed to think where this meeting might lead but he couldn't just walk away and leave it. 'Would you let me give you dinner one night?'

'I'd like that very much indeed.' She added with her first concession to conventions which he believed she despised:

'Harry had very few friends and I've fewer. I'm going to be rather a lonely woman.'

'Not for long, I hope.'

'I'm extremely choosey. I chose Harry and I never regretted it.'

'Would Thursday evening suit you, then?'

'I've no engagements now. I'm grateful .'

She gave him the name of a local restaurant where the cooking was solid and unpretentious. Both were silent as they neared the station. He asked her permission to light a cigar and as he leant to his right to avoid a draught he could see in the driver's mirror briefly. It was only a glimpse as he straightened quickly but his scalp had begun to crawl in excitement. It had been a perfectly ordinary car behind them but this had happened to Charles Russell before. He hadn't evidence, which he liked to decide on, nor even a wholly convincing guess why anyone should think it worth while to tag him from Penny Maxim's flat. But he'd been shadowed before and more than once and Charles Russell had developed an instinct. It had saved his life twice and he trusted it blindly.

He said to Penny: 'Stop. Draw in.'

It had the ring of an authentic order and she did what he said without thought or question. The other car had stopped behind them.

'I shan't be there a moment. Please wait.'

He got out and walked back to the second car. It held two men, rather nondescript Indians. Russell opened the door and looked them over. They weren't the type to risk physical violence.

'Gentlemen, I can save you some trouble. I have been calling on Mrs. Penny Maxim who is the daughter of Sir William Fenwick. I am now returning to London by train. No doubt you know my address. Good day.'

He banged the door with something less than deference and returned to Penny Maxim.

'Trouble?'

'Not really. A silly tailing. Phoney.'
'You played it pretty cool.'
'How else?'
She said in the contemporary jargon but with a tiny catch in her warm contralto:
'Coolies turn me on.'
'Translate.'
'I'll do no such thing. You work it out.'
He looked at her. 'It's a compliment?'
'More.'

3

Charles Russell went home and put his feet up. He had the gift of instant sleep and had needed it, and he slept with all of a child's intensity. But when he woke at his usual time he started to think. When he'd made an excuse to leave Penny Maxim he had done so for an excellent reason; he had needed to consider calmly where their meeting could conceivably lead him.

That he soon decided firmly. It might lead him where he didn't wish to go. He hadn't asked for a hand in this high-stake game and was determined that one shouldn't be dealt to him. He'd been drawn into more than one adventure since retirement had ended his active career, and these he had not objected to: indeed he had in a quiet way relished them. Moreover he shared with most normal men a horror of any traffic in drugs. But there was something about the present scenario which set the alarm bells jangling peremptorily. It was the smell of a private revenge and he shied from it. A gang of unauthorized vigilantes. . . .

He wouldn't touch them if they offered a million.

His respect for the law was not exaggerated and he'd done much in his working life well outside it. The state had paid his salary though it hadn't appeared on any Vote, but if he put a foot wrong he'd be broken mercilessly. That had been the unspoken bargain. Very well, so he'd bent the law but not privately. Private revenge was his private anathema.

Nevertheless he was being watched. That didn't frighten him, it had happened before, but it was evidence that someone believed he had taken a hand when he certainly hadn't. Nor did he mean to—never, no never. But he had an engagement with Mrs. Penny Maxim and he didn't intend to stand her up. He seldom stood people up on principle and in any case she'd been very attractive. So he'd spend a very pleasant evening and there the affair would pleasantly end. He wasn't going in with that lot.

He took another train to Weybridge and a taxi to Penny Maxim's restaurant. It was Italian and he went in doubtfully. Italian restaurants in the London suburbs could reach depths of really dreadful cooking unequalled even by Cypriot immigrants. But he went in and looked around, reassured. The lights were discreet but not tiresomely dim, there were no candles stuck in grease-caked bottles.

'*Siamo in due.*'

'*Sissignor.* Of course you have reserved?'

'Of course. The name is Russell. I rang two days ago.' He had indeed done so, he never took chances.

He was led to a table and ordered a drink, then he looked at the menu, again reassured. It didn't look fussy, it might even be excellent. No pasta, he thought—most women were scared of it—but a tray had gone by with some real *mortadella*. *Mortadella*, then, and of course black olives. After that veal, done with cheese and spinach, and he hoped that the veal would not be English. If this place was as good as its ambience said it was they'd have brought it in from Holland where it was best. Wine, Valpolicella—Chiantis were doubtful. The sweet he would leave to Penny Maxim, assuming that she wanted one and he guessed that she very probably wouldn't. His impression of Mrs. Penny Maxim was a woman who would know about food, in which case he would pay her the compliment of not fussing her over what she wanted, but ordering a sound meal and presenting it.

As he finished the order she came through the door. He rose and took her fur coat, a good one. Harry Maxim had been a successful craftsman and in any case she was Fenwick's daughter. As he slid her chair under she said conversationally:

'I was afraid you wouldn't come.'

'Why not?' He might have been offended but wasn't.

'I've had time to think since we met at the funeral. You're Charles Russell and you're also retired. And what I am is an undesirable.'

'Your choice of word,' he said.

'I'll stay with it.' She ate the *mortadella* sensibly, not cutting it up but using a fork, spitting the olive stones out discreetly. 'I think you've been called on by Lesley King.'

'How did you know that?'

'He told me. Father hired him and I'm in this with Father. So now you see why I'm undesirable. I was always very fond of my half-brother, though his mother hated the sight of me and always made any meeting difficult. On top of that I've lost my husband working for my father and Lesley. That wasn't Lesley's fault, just bad luck, and in any case I'd agreed it with Harry. But I'm naturally bitterer now than ever.'

Charles Russell didn't answer this. He poured her more wine and waited. Fruitfully.

'Am I talking too much? It's a great relief.'

'Not at all. Please go on.'

The veal and the fresh spinach were cooling but it was evident she had little appetite. 'So you were walking along the street to your flat and my husband's body damned near killed you. You knew him but you kept your mouth shut.'

'King wanted me to keep it shut.'

'Wouldn't you have kept it shut anyway?'

'Hypothetical question.'

She said with a flicker of irritation: 'I know that men hate them but there it is.' She toyed with the spinach but not the veal. 'But yet you came here to attend the funeral.'

'You know I once employed your husband. I felt I had an obligation.'

'You're a very strange man.'

'I had very strange work.'

Her food had congealed in a shapeless misery and she looked at Charles Russell in quick apology. 'It isn't that it isn't nice, it's simply I can't eat a thing. You can see I'm on a private rack.'

'I'm told that in Inquisition days the man on the rack could demand and get food. That is, if he felt like food, which I doubt. But there were rules of a sort and the Dominicans kept them.'

For the first time that evening she managed a smile. 'May I have a little cheese, the *Bel Paese*.'

As she nibbled at the cheese she asked: 'May I call you Charles?'

'I'd be very much flattered.'

'What do you know of the drug traffic, Charles?'

'Not very much—such men weren't my target. But sometimes the lines of sight would cross.'

'Then I'll tell you what Lesley King told me.' She took out a cigarette and he lit it. 'In practice a drug ring is more like a ladder, and all of them have at least four rungs. At the bottom are the simple pedlars—pushers I rather think they call them. They're loathsome by any human rating but the men on the rungs above are worse. Worse because they know more and accept it. Above the pushers are the men who distribute from the man who handles the latest consignment, and at the top of the pile is the great provider, fount and origin of the whole vile business. We even know his name. It's Manerji.'

'And your father intends to smash this ladder?'

'The ladder but chiefly the man at the top of it. And on this ladder of ours it goes like this. We know that Sen is the collecting point—my husband lost his life trying to prove it—and those Sikhs are almost surely the runners. Manerji must be somewhere in India and he's the one we really want.'

He didn't ask questions but ordered coffee and brandy. Over them, as he'd hoped, she went on.

'Lesley King was in the Drug Squad once and anything he says is probably right. He says that drug barons run much to type in the sense that they're not solely drug barons. Almost always they're big in something else, gambling and prostitution perhaps, and often in legitimate business.'

'So first you've got to find him?'

'We shall.'

'And then you intend to destroy him?'

'Of course.' She hadn't raised her voice a semi-tone.

'Quite an assignment,' Charles Russell said blandly.

'Oh, you needn't imagine anything foolish, no gunmen sent out to Mother India. We'll have to get him here in England. Nibble at his existing ladder. Chop off the lower rungs. Force his hand.'

'You think that would bring him to England?'

'What else?'

Charles Russell finished his brandy thoughtfully. 'You said "Nibble at his existing ladder". *Suppose that he starts nibbling yours.*'

'What was that?' She was startled. He'd meant to startle her.

'Consider the point of view of this Big Boy. If he's anything like what you seem to think he'll look at the English papers at least, which weren't reticent on your brother's death. So he'll know about that and who was his father — a wealthy, determined and vengeful man. The next bit he will have learnt from Sen, and if I were in his shoes I wouldn't like it. A man is caught by a broken safe at a moment when it's full of heroin. What else he knows we can only guess, but its certain he'll have other sources than Sen. If he's half as big as I think you're suggesting, I wouldn't care to bet a penny that he doesn't know all about you and King — that you have the father you happen to have and that King has been hired to serve that father. Why should he wait for you to move?'

'I hadn't thought of that,' she said.

'Then I suggest that you all three think of it urgently.'

'You think we're in danger?'

'I think you're vulnerable.'

'And you?' she asked.

'I don't quite follow.'

'You were out in the street when Harry fell.'

'With every reason to be there quite innocently. But a careful Big Boy mightn't leave it at that. He might check my contacts afterwards. As he did.'

'Then have you been followed here tonight?'

'I don't know that but I didn't *feel* it. I've an instinct but it isn't infallible.'

'I have instincts too and mostly trust them.'

'You're a woman. You have better reason to.'

'Since you offer an opening, here it comes. What do you think of Lesley King?'

'I think he's very good at his job. I think your father chose well to employ him. But I'm very glad I'm not his enemy.'

'You wouldn't consider becoming his friend?' She lit her next cigarette for herself. For once he simply hadn't noticed. In his astonishment he said almost curtly:

'What can you mean?'

'I'm asking you to join us, Charles.'

'Join your father and yourself and King? To smash the drug traffic of a man in India?'

'Don't you loathe the whole business?'

'Of course I do. What astounds me is why you think I could help. I'm no longer young and drugs weren't my country.'

'You're wise and you've an enormous experience.'

'But I haven't what makes you all tick—the motive. You talked about nibbling away at their ladder and I suggested they'd counter-nibble at you. "Nibble", indeed—an extraordinary word.' He leant across, caught her eyes and held them. 'You talked about experience so I'll give you mine for the little it's worth. There's big money on both sides of this, your father's at one end, Indian money the other. And big money can buy many things. It can buy kidnappings and muggings—and death. Remember that while you've still the time.'

She said very coolly: 'We've thought of that.'

'Then I've nothing more to say. I'm sorry.'

'Would you talk to Lesley King again?'

'I would if your father sent him. Not otherwise.'

'You're very determined.'

'I'm retired and enjoying it.' It was the truth but he knew that it wasn't the whole of it.

He saw that she was ready to go, so he paid the bill and went to the door with her. At it she said:

'I've a car round the corner so I'll drive you to the station again.'

'That's very kind but I'd rather walk.'

'I've offended you,' she said with a smile.

'No, not at all—you mustn't think it. But I've eaten a lot and I fancy the exercise. There's an hour to the last train. That's plenty.'

He walked with her to her car and saw her in. As she settled she asked: 'Shall we meet again?'

'As a woman I would very much hope so. As a member of what amounts to a gang I must hope that I never see you again.'

'You're very frank.'

'It leaves a clean wound.'

She started the engine but leant out of the window. 'We *are* going to meet again,' she said.

'Another instinct?' he asked her vanishing back but no answer came back on the wind of her passing.

He began to walk towards the station, swinging his arms and moving briskly. There was nobody about and few cars, and he was surprised at a roar of engines behind him. Motorcycles, he thought, and big ones—boys showing off on ton-up monsters. He turned to look and there they were, six of them in two lines of three.

He stood still intending to let them pass, hoping that their exhausts wouldn't poison him. They came closer, tightening up the formation, swerving suddenly towards the pavement and boxing him. Opposite him the leader signalled and the first file bumped their front wheels up the kerb. The other three had spread out in the road, one to the left, another right, and the last stationed neatly between the first two. Russell thought of some loutish jest but dismissed it. There was a feeling of practice, almost drill. And running was clearly out of the question. If he ran for it they would cut him down.

He looked behind him quickly. Old house. Old Victorian house painted white. No matter. Probably flats by now. Not important. But there was a basement around what had once been the kitchens, the drop to it maybe ten or twelve feet.

Russell backed against the railing which guarded it, feeling behind him. Yes, a gate. A gate meant steps to the basement well, where motorcycles couldn't follow him.

He felt again. Gate locked. Someone laughed.

He faced the front file of cyclists silently. The white-painted house reflected their headlights. He saw helmets and goggles but nothing else. They'd tied scarves across the rest of their faces.

The leader raised his hand again and the front file revved their engines savagely. Their back wheels came up the kerb.

Russell jumped for it. The railing was four feet high but not spiked and Russell put a hand on and vaulted. He was active still but no longer an athlete and the drop had been increased by the vault. He landed in an untidy heap, sick with a sudden pain in an ankle. Above him he heard a derisive laugh, then the noise of powerful engines fading. He tried to get up but failed. He collapsed.

When he came to the basement window was open, a man's head thrusting out aggressively. It wore a clerical collar none too clean and an air of distaste for unseemly happenings.

'What's the meaning of this?'

'We'll consider that later, but I assure you I'm neither drunk, or doped. For the moment, if you'd be good enough, I'd be grateful if you'd call an ambulance.'

Charles Russell woke next morning uneasily, conscious of strange time and surroundings. He normally woke at half past seven but by the light in his room it was fully midday and the room said 'hospital', maybe 'nursing home'. He looked round and confirmed what was so far impression. A coloured nurse sat on a hard chair, knitting.

Black but comely, he thought. All properly biblical.

When she noticed his eyes were open she came to him. 'How are you feeling?'

'It might be worse. What's this place, by the way?'

'St. Agatha's nursing home.'

'And where's St. Agatha's?'

'Here in Weybridge.'

It was beginning to come back to him but for the moment his returning mind was concerned with the immediate present. 'Am I badly hurt?'

'That's for the doctor.'

'Come on, my dear. Why not tell me straight?'

She hesitated but said at last: 'I think you're a very lucky chentleman. You were concussed when they brought you in but not badly. We had to quieten you but there's nothing in that. Then you've broken a bone in your foot but we've fixed it.'

'Plaster?' he asked anxiously. He hated to be immobile for long.

'No, it's not too bad, we were able to strap it. You should be walking about almost normally soon.'

'Better than nothing. May I have tea?'

'And a little to eat?'

'No thank you. Not yet.'

He was half way through the pale sweet tea when he realized that it tasted odd.

. . . They certainly believe in sedation.

But he finished it: the doctor knew best. 'May I smoke?'

She said a little doubtfully: 'There were cigars in your coat but you can't have those here.'

'Then give me a cigarette.'

She produced one. She leant over him to light it neatly. She smelt of very clean starched linen.

She stood watching him professionally, making sure that he didn't set fire to the bed. He was still pretty shaky, not fit to talk, especially to the plain clothes policeman who was anxiously waiting below to do so. When he'd smoked enough of the cigarette she crushed out what was left in an ashtray. 'Now you'd better go to sleep again.' She gave him her warm and friendly smile. Her teeth were very big and very white.

. . . All the better to eat you with. Now why did I think of that? I'm doped.

He slept again and woke in the evening. The nurse was still there and a white-coated doctor. The doctor said crisply:

'No talking yet, or none that isn't strictly necessary. But there's a policeman downstairs who's been waiting some time. Do you feel up to him?'

'Yes, of course.'

'Then I'll give him exactly five minutes. No more.'

The policeman came in and sat down quietly. The nurse was still with them. She was conscientious as well as pretty and was holding her watch in her hand. She was timing it.

'Colonel Charles Russell?'

Russell nodded.

'But I haven't come her to take a statement, sir. That will have to come later but for the moment we know most of it.'

'May I know how?'

'I don't see why not. There was a lady at a window opposite. She saw motorcycles attacking a man. The man jumped over a railing and didn't return. She rang the police.'

He was thinking how often it happened in fact. The road deserted, the street lamps indifferent, and opposite, in an unlighted window, some sleepless lonely woman staring at nothing. Every street in every town in England had one at least and often more. They sat there and watched in desperation till they saw some sign of life.

Or of death. No, that wasn't a stupid exaggeration.

'But there's one thing I must ask you at once. Did you recognize anyone?'

'I'm sorry, but no. They had leather jackets and heavy boots and some of them wore a sort of bodybelt. But they had helmets on their heads and goggles, and scarves round the lower parts of their faces.'

'A pity,' the policeman said. 'A great pity. It's going to be very hard to trace them.' He looked at the nurse who held up one finger. 'You see, those bikes were not their own. They were found abandoned ten miles away and they'd been stolen from a club in South London. So had the gear for that matter. Difficult.'

The nurse had risen and so did the policeman. 'Then that's all for the moment, sir, and thank you. They'll ring us when you feel up to a statement.'

For the third time that day Charles Russell slept.

He woke next day at his normal time, feeling much better and very hungry. The nurse wasn't there, but he rang the bell and when she appeared with her wide warm smile, 'I'm ravenous,' Charles Russell told her.

'What would you like?'

'A damned great breakfast.'

As he was eating his generous breakfast the nurse said softly: 'Another visitor.'

'What sort of visitor?'

'Very rich.'

'How do you know?'

'I saw the car. Brand new Rolls-Royce and chauffeur-driven.'

'That impressed you?' he asked.

'Of course it did.' The question had clearly surprised her greatly.

'There are people who think Rolls-Royces vulgar.'

'I think that's silly. I'd love to have one.'

'Then you're a sensible girl as well as beautiful. I would guess that the owner's name is Fenwick since I haven't a lot of friends with Rolls-Royces. When I've finished my breakfast please have him shown up.'

'You're up to it now?'

'I'm feeling fine.'

Willy Fenwick came in and Russell thought he looked terrible. 'I was talking to my daughter last night. I can't forgive myself so I won't ask yours.'

. . . Shaky syntax but he still looks shaky.

'First King calls on you without my authority.'

'He told me the call was his own idea.'

'Then you go to my son-in-law's funeral. Nice of you.' He left it at that and went on dourly. 'Where you meet my daughter. Did you know she was that?'

'Not till she asked me back to her flat.'

'Which I wouldn't have allowed if I'd felt up to being present. My private intentions—you know what I mean—are my own and nobody else's whatever. I don't want old friends involved in any way.'

'Am I involved?'

'You're here on your back.'

'And your daughter told you what I told her? Allow me to dot the Is and cross the Ts. All that happened was somebody thought I was dangerous, so when your son-in-law fell out of that window that somebody had my movements shadowed. I went to Harry Maxim's funeral because I thought it a proper thing to do, but afterwards I went to his widow's flat and the lady turns out to be your daughter. I didn't know that but somebody thought I did. So he arranged to have me frightened off.'

36

Sir William said on a note of surprise: 'You don't think they were trying to kill you?'

'There are a dozen ways of killing a man, an unarmed man in an empty street. No, they were trying to scare me. They did.'

'I don't know how to apologize.'

'Don't.'

'And I've another and much greater regret. I told you I talked to my daughter yesterday and she told me that she'd asked you to join us. That was an impertinence.'

'Was it? Your daughter's a very attractive woman and a type which men of my age fall for helplessly. Moreover such women know it perfectly. "Impertinence" isn't a word appropriate.'

'Nevertheless, I'm sorry.'

'You needn't be. I am ready to join you.'

There was a moment of unrelenting silence. Russell was thinking his private thoughts. It was curious how the mind worked in crisis, the mind of a man no longer a youth. He'd been assaulted and put into hospital, damn them; he was every bit as furious as a younger man would surely be. Who might well have joined up with Fenwick in anger when he wouldn't have dreamed of joining him otherwise. But an older head saw it rather differently. You went into crazy schemes like Fenwick's in the coldest of blood or not at all. Anger was a very poor counsellor and of anger Russell was purged and innocent. He felt almost no emotion whatever, content, as a good determinist should be, to float with an ineluctable tide. And if another man had challenged him, obliged him to use the language of reason, he had, after all, a respectable motive:

'The Drug Squad is entirely competent but in this case they'd be hamstrung politically. You know what these people are—they're diplomats. They may be overpaid messenger boys but they all stick together to protect what they've got. There'd be an instant closing of ranks, a curtain, and that curtain would be put down by the Foreign

Office.'

Fenwick started to light a cigar: Russell stopped him. 'We're not allowed those in here.'

Fenwick put it in its case and considered; he had something to say and was finding it difficult. He felt he owed an explanation and finally it came out awkwardly.

'So I'm going to risk a breach of good manners, a breach of consideration, really.' He hesitated but got it out. 'Have you seen a man die of heroin—the last stages?'

'By the mercy of God I never have.'

'An only son at that.'

'I understand.'

'But you don't begin to understand. The frustration, the sense of utter helplessness. The efficient and helpful police machine but stalemate in three moves. Intolerable.' He stood up suddenly, trembling visibly. 'It's a racket and I'm going to smash it.'

'Take it easy, Willy.'

'Easy to you, old friend. You know nothing. I can guess what you're thinking and guess it right. You don't approve of private vendettas. I dare say you killed a score of men but you did it as an official. Clean hands. Well I haven't got clean hands, I don't want them. I don't care what I do or whom I employ.'

'You're going to have a stroke, you know.'

Fenwick fought for control and finally won it. He sat down again, this time too heavily. His breath was coming in gasps; he wiped his face.

Charles Russell decided to change the subject. 'Amongst other things you were talking of people. The people you employ, I mean.'

Fenwick was almost back to normal. 'For the moment I've only one. Lesley King.'

'Your daughter mentioned Lesley King.'

'Did she ask questions?'

'They always ask questions. I told her the truth. I said that I thought you'd chosen wisely.'

'No more than that?'

'You bounce to and fro quite a bit, dear Willy. One moment uncomfortably close to hysteria, the next the tycoon firing ruthless questions.'

'I'm sorry again but I have to know. Was that all you told her, Charles?'

'It was not. I told her I was very glad that King was not my personal enemy. But then I wouldn't want as an enemy any man who was deeply committed on anything. What Lesley King hates is all traffic in drugs. That makes him a very good servant to you but to me it's a warning in letters of fire.'

'You're saying I shouldn't trust him?'

'Not at all. I'm saying that for different reasons he's as crazy as you are and maybe more. That doubles the danger of something foolish before I get out of here and can guide you. I hope that doesn't sound pompous.'

'A trifle.' Fenwick's smile belied the bite of the words; he added: 'You really mean to join us?'

'Didn't I say so?'

'I couldn't believe it.'

'But if you want a motive here it is. What riles me about this particular drug traffic is the fact that it's being run by diplomats. That isn't in the rules. It's cheating.'

Sir William Fenwick rose, now steadily. 'I don't know how to thank you.'

'Don't.'

'Come to dinner when you're out of here.'

'Make it a good one, you owe me that. And if you can hold your hand till we've talked it over it would help towards my peace of mind.'

'I'll see what can be done.'

He took his leave.

Charles Russell dropped back on the nursing home's pillows. . . . 'I'll see what can be done'. . . . Not a promise.

. . . I must get out of here and get out fast.

The same nurse arrived next morning, still smiling. 'Another visitor,' she told Russell.

'With Rolls?'

'A Mini this time.' She gave him a card.

Charles Russell read it, his spirits falling. It was a man he knew at his club but not well. In point of fact he avoided him nimbly since he was not only a diplomat but a recognized bore.

'Could you say I'm not fit to see him?'

'If you wish.'

Russell considered, then shook his head. That too would be a sort of cheating. 'Bring him and let him say his piece but rescue me when I ring the bell.'

Ivan Pendell came in and Russell waved at a chair. Pendell was carefully rather than elegantly dressed, his manner the sort of bonhomous-official which was nowadays standard for British diplomats.

'I hope you're getting on all right.'

'They tell me I'll recover this time.'

It was something short of handsomely welcoming, but Charles Russell had begun to feel pain. Whatever analgesics they'd given him had started to wear off, and so far they hadn't offered others. 'I'd rather you came to the point at once. In any case they won't let you stay long.'

Pendell began with a ponderous skill, an elephant treading on egg shells and proud of it, stating facts but without commitment. Sir William Fenwick had lost a son in circumstances which had caused him distress, and was known to have taken it very badly. Charles Russell was a friend of Fenwick and in the circumstances that might prove embarrassing.

'Embarrassing to whom?' Russell asked.

Surprisingly Pendell answered: 'To us.'

'The Foreign Office?'

'Commonwealth Relations side.'

'Would you care to be more explicit?'

'Need I?' He went off again in *oratio obliqua*. Russell had been walking home when a man had fallen from an Indian's window. That man had been a safebreaker, as had been admitted at the inquest openly, and he had broken the Indian's safe before he was caught. Now looking at those facts dispassionately. . . .

Charles Russell wasn't feeling dispassionate. He disliked this man and mistrusted his trade, and his foot had begun to hurt rather badly. He decided to hurry it up and said:

'That Indian shared your profession.'

'Yes.' Pendell hesitated but couldn't resist it. 'Of course he was a good deal my junior.'

'An Attaché and, I now learn, an odd one. I've heard of Military and Naval Attachés, Labour and Press Attachés—dozens. But I'd not heard before of an Attaché for the Environment. Now what do you make of that?'

'That the Indians are interested in studying the Environment.' It came back as smooth as a good mayonnaise.

'Are there others of that ilk in London?'

'Not that I know of.'

'So Sen's unique?'

Ivan Pendell nodded; he didn't like it. He was experienced and a long way from stupid, but somewhere he had lost the initiative. This man on the bed had him going backwards and he wouldn't give him time to reform.

'So I'll tell you what I think for what it's worth. I've heard of unusual jobs before and all of them had one thing in common. That was a very powerful patron. *And powerful patrons demand strange services.*'

'You may well be right but is it the point?'

'What *is* the point?'

'Our relations with India.'

'What would India do to help us in a pinch?'

The other said with a stiff formality: 'Bismark has been dead a long time.' He'd been hoping to recover some ground but instead he made Russell lose his temper. It was something Russell did extremely seldom but when it happened he could be alarmingly formidable. He said in a cold, clear, dangerous voice:

'So if India left the Commonwealth . . .?'

'I do not care to speculate, Colonel.'

'Nor do I need to since I *know* what would happen. A thousand officials would lose their employment.'

'You are being something less than helpful.'

'I know no motive to offer you help.' Charles Russell rang the bell for the nurse. 'I'm sorry,' he said in his normal manner. 'If I've been less than polite it's because I'm in pain.'

The black nurse came in and stood demurely.

'Will you please see this gentleman out to his car?'

Pendell rose but made no move to go. He stared at Russell hard, the mask dropping. 'I believe you have a generous pension.'

Charles Russell drew a very deep breath. A voice which didn't sound like his own asked:

'Is that a threat?'

'There are certain rules.'

There was another spasm in Russell's foot, an orgasm where he kept his urbanity. To the nurse he said: 'Please leave the room.' To Pendell he snarled:

'And you eff off.'

TWO

TWO

1

Immobilized in St. Agatha's Nursing Home, Russell was recovering quickly, but not quickly enough to prevent what he'd feared. Which was intemperate action by his other three partners. For Fenwick and King and Penny Maxim were gathered in what was a council of war.

Fenwick was saying: 'I'm glad he's come in. He's experienced and he pulls many strings. But he hasn't lost a son or a husband. He wants us to wait and see what happens.'

'But,' Penny Maxim said, 'we simply can't afford to wait. You remember what I told you he said to me? I told him we meant to destroy their ladder, a rung at a time till we reached the top, and what he told me was to watch our own step. Why should they just sit back and take punishment? I'd guess that he sees it in military terms, or perhaps as things happened in the Security Executive. Attack by us, then the counter by them.'

Sir William turned to Lesley King. 'You see it like that too?'

'It begins to look a bit like that. We put in a safebreaker to search Sen's flat, and the frighteners promptly get put on to Russell. That was jumping to conclusions no doubt—as it happened Russell wasn't with us then—but the fact of the strong reaction remains.'

'Which on Russell's hypothesis means it's our turn for movement.'

'Yes,' King said, 'I think it is.'

'Then what do you plan to do?'

King considered. He hated sharing his plans with anyone, but Fenwick held the purse strings—money talked. 'The orthodox course is to start at the bottom.'

'The pushers?' Fenwick asked.

'The pushers. But I don't think smashing the pushers would take us far. They're a hydra-headed people in practice—I learnt that when I was in the Drug Squad. You break one lot and others spring up pretty quickly. Moreover it works like a wartime Resistance, they don't know the names of the men above them. They know where to collect from a drop but after that they're on their own. You can interrogate them till you're sick and tired but they're telling the truth when they say they know nothing.' King shook his head. 'No, not the pushers.'

'Then what's the target?'

'The next rung upwards.'

'The runners?' It was Penny Maxim.

'Those two Sikhs who work under Sen—that's right. Both of them serve the High Commission. One is a driver, the other a guard. Their names are on some list or other but they haven't the almost absolute privilege of a diplomat with credentials like Sen. More important, the ranks wouldn't close to protect them. They'd be just naughty boys who'd been caught in a racket. Their superiors would wring their hands, perhaps they might even apologize privately, but they wouldn't start pushing the Whitehall bells. No, they'd throw them to the wolves discreetly.'

'But I want more than that,' Willy Fenwick said.

'You pay handsomely to get it, sir.' There was perhaps a hint of acidity but it was a very long way short of impertinence. 'So I've been able to buy pretty good information. The drop is in Leicester, that's almost certain, though we don't know exactly where it is. But we know that there's been a fresh consignment. Within a day or two they must get it out or their pushers will start to go elsewhere. This isn't the only drug racket operating.'

'I see. And then?'

'Those Sikhs are being watched day and night. That's expensive with first class men but you're generous. So I'll let them go to Leicester and follow them. I'll let them dump at their drop so we'll know where it is, then I'll make a quick call to official friends. You can be certain they'll be extremely grateful.'

Sir William Fenwick ground his cigar out. 'An objection,' he said. 'I think an objection. If they've been to their drop they'll be clean as whistles.'

'Oh no they won't. They'll be carrying plenty. Not what they dumped at the drop, but plenty.'

There was a palpable silence which lasted some time. Presently Penny Maxim said: 'Splendid.' Sir William Fenwick said nothing at all.

The two Sikhs had done it often before but V. S. Sen, conscientious and clerkly, was taking them through it all again.

'You collect at eight o'clock in the morning when I'll still be here to open the safe.'

Neither of them spoke; they knew it.

'Then a taxi to St Pancras station and the five past ten to Leicester. Right?'

'That's right,' the older Sikh said wearily.

'You take ordinary bags but nothing expensive. If anyone gets into conversation you are fitters who've lost your jobs in London and are looking for others up in the Midlands. But don't talk more than you have to.'

'We won't.' In point of fact one had better English than he'd chosen to expose to Sen.

'Then a car will meet you at Leicester as usual. Stand outside with your luggage and wait till it hails you. It will take you to where you need to go.'

They left at a quarter past eight next morning, and in a bed-sitter of a flat almost opposite a man slipped quickly downstairs and into the street. King had told Fenwick he'd hired the best and this man stayed behind the two Sikhs unobtrusively, black-hatted with rolled umbrella and newspaper, the typical office worker on his way. He stayed there for maybe two hundred yards till the Sikhs found a taxi. He quickened his pace. He heard them give the order—St Pancras. A tobacconist was open already and he ran to it and telephoned King.

'They're in a taxi to St. Pancras station.'

'That fits with having their drop in Leicester. Take a taxi yourself and wait at the station. By the board with the timetables—left as you enter. If I don't make it follow alone.'

But the Sikhs hadn't rushed things and King made it comfortably. Leaning against the board with the timetables was a neatly dressed man who was reading a newspaper.

'Good morning, Dick.'

'Good morning, Lesley. Next train to Leciester at five past ten. They've bought their tickets and I've bought ours.' He handed one to Lesley King.

'Where are they now?'

The other man pointed. 'Over there in something called the Stirrup Cup Bar. But they won't be drinking stirrup cups, they'll be swilling down their tea as usual.'

Lesley King grinned. 'You've done your homework.'

'I've had plenty of time to do it in. What do we do now?'

'We go with them.' King looked at his watch. 'There's another twelve minutes. I'll watch that so-called bar while you case the train.'

Dick wandered away to look at the train, but King stayed leaning and seemingly bored, trying to look like a man with a date and succeeding. St. Pancras wasn't his favourite station. The inside was fine by any standard, the single span of the great glassed arch, the splendid old ironwork supporting it gracefully. But the building outside made him sweatily queasy. It was fashionable to apologize for it and there were even people who praised it openly. But King was a man of simple tastes and he didn't much care for the gothic revival.

Dick had been casing the train with some interest for he had a feeling for trains as King had for buildings. A queue was forming outside the barrier, being held there till the cleaners had finished. There were two porters sweeping up the litter. Both of them had rheumy colds and one of them spat on the platform copiously. Dick returned to Lesley King and said:

'It's an Inter-City. Not too bad.' For the first time he looked at the bar directly. 'They're coming out at last.'

'So I see.'

The Sikhs joined the tail of the queue and waited, and the other two slipped in behind them. They were carrying suitcases, not very big ones. The ticket collector raised the barrier and the queue began to shuffle forward. Dick and Lesley King went with it.

Half way up the rake the Sikhs stopped. They looked at a No Smoking notice, then climbed into the carriage quickly. King began to follow them but Dick held up a hand in instant protest.

'No Smoking, that one.' He smoked rather heavily.

'Of course it is.'

'And why of course?'

'Sikhs never smoke—it's against their religion. They'll do most other things for money, damn them, but you won't catch a Sikh with a cigarette.'

'I didn't know that.'

'You were never a policeman.'

'Eighty-five minutes to Leicester. I'll bear it.'

They followed the Sikhs and sat down opposite. It was an open carriage, the seats in pairs. There were tables between them and these were down. There was a buffet on this train but no service.

When they were through the northern suburbs, King folded his newspaper and smiled at the Sikhs. He looked out of the window indifferently. The train had begun to gather speed.

'This is quite a good train,' he said.

'It is nice.'
'Do you use it often?'
'No, never before.'
Unnecessary lie. Bad mark.

The Sikh looked at his companion uneasily. He would much have preferred to travel in silence, but since this chatty stranger wished to talk it would look odd to sit in a stubborn silence.

'Have you been in England long?'
'About a year,' the Sikh said promptly.
Lie number two. They've been here much longer.

The Sikh had made his mind up suddenly. Since he had to talk he would say his piece, the rigmarole arranged with Sen.

'We are going to Leicester to look for work. We had work in London but we lost it unfairly.'
'Do you have a trade?'
'I beg your pardon?'
'Do you have, well, any sort of skill?'
'We are both of us fitters.'
'Then you shouldn't have too much difficulty wherever you choose to look for a job.'

But the second Sikh had broken in. There was a mutter of colloquial Punjabi and both men rose with polite forced smiles. 'And now I think we will take some tea.' They rose and took their luggage with them.

Still fifty minutes to go to Leicester. Third mistake.

They went down the gangway carrying their bags and when they had gone Dick said contemptuously:

'They live on tea. It rots their guts. Do we follow them?'
'No point in that. The buffet car is behind this carriage. Even if we tried we could hardly lose them.'

Outside the station they formed queue for a taxi, the two Sikhs three or four couples in front. The moving file of approaching cabs was broken by a private car. It was an old-fashioned Daimler, enormous and stately, the kind which a Queen had once sat in magnificently. King said softly to Dick:

'And that'll be theirs.'

The Sikhs let three taxis go by them to others and then, as the Daimler stopped, moved towards it. The driver got down and opened the door for them.

'We'll take the next taxi.'

'*I wouldn't try it.*'

The voice was behind them, assured but casual. Lesley King felt the gun in his liver. He didn't move.

'I'm not alone. My friend has yours covered.'

The voice was speaking excellent English but with an accent which Lesley King could recognize. 'A Chinaman,' he said without meaning to.

'A Chinaman is a left-hander's googly. I much prefer to be called Chinese. Hong Kong if you insist on it, and please don't use that word again.'

The driver of the old-fashioned Daimler shut the door on the Sikhs and moved away.

'I propose to stay here till that car is well clear. After that you may take any taxi you fancy.'

There are people all around us. He might not risk it.

The voice read the thought. 'I would try nothing foolish. For me it would be far more unpleasant to let you follow that car than serve a sentence.'

The four of them were bunched close together and a taxi-driver looked at them curiously. But there were other fares behind them. He drove on.

A minute went by, then the Chinese spoke again. 'We are going now. Don't look round or follow. You will give us three minutes, then do as you please.'

King felt the gun slide away from his liver, but he said to Dick beside him: 'Don't move. They'll slip away in an organized leapfrog, one covering the other all the way.'

When three minutes had gone he moved at last. 'I need a drink and I need it badly.'

They went to a bar and ordered whisky. Dick took a second; he was visibly shaken.

'Stuck up by a bloody Chinese.' he said.

'It was very slick work—those men were pros. That Daimler is anywhere in the town by now, or perhaps it didn't go to Leicester.' King thought, then made his mind up quickly. 'You stay here the night for what that's worth, just in case there's any sort of development. I don't think there will be but perhaps we should cover it. I'm going back to London.'

'Okay.'

The regal old car had gone some way, the Sikhs in the back seats with their bags. At first the driver had chatted amiably but after a while he wound the partition up.

'I've never seen a car like this.'

'It must be twenty years old and probably more. They don't make anything like it today.'

'But comfortable. Very posh.' The Sikh pointed at a rack of decanters. 'Those were for drinks,' he said unnecessarily.

It was a relief to be able to speak his own language and he chattered on briskly, annoying the other. 'A speaking tube, too. Not even a telephone. You blow down it first,' he explained, 'and it whistles. Then the driver takes the whistle out and puts the earpiece to his ear to hear you.'

'Be quiet,' the other Sikh said. 'We need to be fresh.'

He looked out of the window and suddenly frowned. 'This isn't the way we usually go.'

'Perhaps there's a road up somewhere.'

'Perhaps.'

They travelled maybe another mile, then the elder Sikh said: 'This isn't right.' He rapped on the glass partition hard. The driver didn't turn his head.

'Try that speaking tube.'

'I think I will.'

The elder Sikh reached across to take it, pulling out the plug and blowing. But it didn't whistle, it blew back in his face. He was conscious of a very faint mist, of a smell which he had never smelt. Then he fell off his seat on the floor of the car. The other Sikh moved to help, but fell too.

The driver kept on driving steadily. A man with a knowledge of midland towns would have guessed that they were approaching water, one of the old and decaying canals which threaded the outskirts of most such cities. The houses were getting more and more squalid, coloured children in the broken streets, and presently there were crumbling factories. The car was going slowly now, picking its way through narrow lanes. It came to a little square and stopped. Here there was nothing, not even children. On three sides of the square were abandoned warehouses. The fourth was open to the black canal.

The driver stopped and waited quietly. Three men came out of a derelict building. All of them were Chinese again.

'Open the doors to let out the gas.'

The driver got down and opened the doors.

They waited a minute. 'It's clear by now. Just give us a hand to get them out.'

The four men pulled out the Sikhs by their legs. They left them in a puddle, face down. The older Sikh had lost his pagaree and the knot of his hair was visible, greying.

'That's all,' the Chinese said. 'You can go.'

The driver climbed back and drove away. Behind him he heard two pistol shots clearly.

Lesley King had returned to his flat and more whisky, for he was facing an embarrassing moment. He'd been made to look an imperial fool and he'd failed in a mission for William Fenwick. The former had rawly scraped his pride, but Fenwick employed him and paid him well; he'd have to report and the sooner the better.

His hand was on the telephone when it rang before he could lift the receiver. It was Dick from Leicester and Dick was excited.

'There *have* been developments.'

'Don't say those Chinese. . . .'

'No nothing like that. It's those Sikhs who've had it. It's all in the evening paper.'

'Read it.'

It was a competent little piece, rather colourful. Two Indians had been found in an old canal. They'd been naked as the day they were born, floating face upwards, their eyes still open. Both had been shot in the back of the head.

A sub-editor, with unusual humanity, had left in the writer's purple passage, the bit about the disused canal, the debris of rotting crates and dead cats, the stench of the filthy oily water. On this water the long hair of the Sikhs had been spreading like some disgusting weed.

'When did they discover this?'

'Round about five in the afternoon.'

'Then stay for the night, but come back tomorrow. Bring tomorrow's Leicester paper. Come to me here as early as possible.'

Lesley King put the receiver down, then telephoned to Sir William Fenwick. 'Can we talk freely?'

'I don't see why not.'

'Something went very wrong at Leicester.'

'You mean your plan failed?'

'No, not quite that.' King gathered himself. 'Those Sikhs are dead.'

'You mean there was some foolish shoot-up?' The voice was incisive and a long way from pleased.

'Can I see you tomorrow morning, sir?'

'Indeed you can. Let us say at eleven.'

'I'll be with you at eleven sharp.'

Lesley King was very punctual next morning, for he had a solid respect for Sir William Fenwick. No doubt his son's death had hit him hard, but he wasn't so broken he'd stand for lateness.

King hadn't so far been to Fenwick's house since their

business had been done in his office, but now he stopped his car in the half-moon drive and looked at it with a cool approval. It was maybe half a mile from the Tennis Club, standing on a little hill, built in Good King Edward's days and built to last at least two centuries. Most of the houses around were now flats, but Fenwick's was till intact and looked it. King nodded in a tolerant envy, for if he'd been rich, which he didn't expect to be, this was the sort of house he'd buy. Not some mansion out in the country, which bored him, but this superbly constructed Edwardian villa in a part of London he rather fancied and where the money, though it clearly existed, had done so for some time and was therefore civilized.

He went up the steps and rang the bell, and Sir William opened the door himself. King looked surprised and Fenwick noticed it, for he said at once:

'I live alone. There's a housekeeper-cook, but she's busy cooking. A woman comes in daily to clean. I tried a man-servant once, but he drove me crazy.'

He led the way into a comfortable study—fine old furniture and a breakfront bookcase full of beautifully bound books which nobody read. King gave him the local morning paper which Dick had brought down from Leicester earlier. The relevant passage was marked in blue pencil, but that had been, in fact, unnecessary. The headline commanded the eye by right.

Fenwick read the two columns and faintly frowned; he said with more than a hint of reserve:

'You mustn't think I'm interfering, far less that these two deaths offend me. They both of them deserved to die—if I didn't think that, we shouldn't be sitting here. But you'd laid out a very different plan, and I don't like it when I'm told one story and something entirely different happens.'

'You weren't, Sir William. I didn't kill them. I and the man I took with me followed those two Sikhs to Leicester. We went on the same train as they did and we intended to

55

do what I told you before, which was to find out their drop and then to plant on them. I had even tipped off an old friend in the Drug Squad. Before whom,' King added a little bitterly, 'I have now had to eat much humble pie.'

'What went wrong?'

'Just about everything. We were standing, waiting outside the station for the car which was certain to pick them up, when we'd follow and do what I told you we meant to. But we never got near them—we were stuck up like children. Guns in our backs like something on telly. The Sikhs drove away and were robbed and killed. Whoever did it must have recognized me—I mean that I worked in the Drug Squad once—and they didn't want any interference.'

Willy Fenwick was staring hard at King. 'I suppose,' he said mildly, 'that your're telling the truth?'

'I'm taking your money.'

'Forgive the question. Then I suppose the intruders were rival Indians.'

'No, sir, they were both Chinese.'

'How do you know?'

'The accent is pretty characteristic and they certainly weren't trying to hide it. One even told me he came from Hong Kong.'

'Did you see their faces?'

'No, we did not—they were both professionals. That's the only salve to my self-respect. They knew their job backwards and did it well. They told us not to turn round. We didn't.'

'It doesn't make sense,' Sir William said. 'Not Indians but Chinese. Inexplicable.'

'Not to me, sir.'

'Then tell me.'

Lesley King lit a cigarette and smoked half of it. Sir William Fenwick waited patiently. King was marshalling his facts in order, which was something Willy Fenwick approved of.

'Those Indians aren't the only ones—the only ones dealing in drugs, I mean.'

'Reluctantly I've got to believe it.'

'The oldest of the other rings is Hong Kong based and Hong Kong run. They've been here for twenty years at least and they don't like competition at all. When it gets too severe they take steps to limit it. It has happened before and will happen again.'

'It's what happened at Leicester?'

'Yes, I would bet on it.'

'From what you tell me it sounds a sensible wager. But there's one thing I don't pretend to follow. You say that this network is based on Hong Kong and has been operating here for some time. Why hasn't it been mopped up by now?'

'Because the Drug Squad ought to be very much bigger. Because that forces it to select its targets. Because those Chinese have their own queer code, which is basically one of moderation.'

'I don't think I'm with you,' Fenwick said.

'Then let's start not with drugs but with drug addiction. There are countries where it's treated compulsorily—you get slapped in a clinic, kill or cure. But that only happens here exceptionally, it doesn't suit our social philosophy. So the addict is referred to a doctor and probably to some social worker. The doctor has no powers of compulsion, the best he can do is try to wean, at any rate with the average case. He cuts down the authorized doses steadily and sometimes it may seem to be working. But as often as not the addict is cheating, he just goes elsewhere for the difference he's missing, and it's less odious when that sort of marginal traffic is run by old hands who are not too greedy.'

William Fenwick polished his glasses carefully. They were perfectly clean and the action was reflex. On the mantel a fine old clock ticked fatly.

'I didn't know that.' He started to ask a question but stopped. Like Russell he knew that the world was imperfect, a choice between lesser evils and great ones. He was shocked though he had said he wouldn't be, but there was nothing to be gained by showing it. 'Go on,' he said. 'There's more to come.'

'Only what I said before. Those Chinese are running a cosy business but our Indian is swamping the market brutally. They would see that as very unfair competition, and being what they are they acted.'

'I think you said those dead Sikhs had been robbed.'

'Of the consignment they were carrying — yes.'

'But another will be coming?'

'I think so. With the profits to be made in drugs our Big Boy is not going to give up easily. He's been wounded but nothing really worse. He's lost a couple of runners but they were trash. The next lot will go to Sen as usual.'

'Who was next on your ladder for treatment anyway?'

'He isn't going to be easy. He moves in a different world from those Sikhs.'

'Do you need more money?'

'Thank you, I've plenty still.'

2

Charles Russell, discharged but slightly limping, had gone to Wimbledon for his promised dinner. It was characteristic of William Fenwick that he didn't press him to state his motives for a change of mind so complete and sudden. He had refused to take any part in their plan: now he had offered to join them. Enough. Instead he offered his private whisky and a précis of events at Leicester. Russell listened in silence, then nodded agreement.

'If King thinks the Chinese did it they probably did. He knows the ways of the world of drugs. I'll take his word.'

'You don't sound very shocked.'

'Should I be shocked? Two corrupt Sikh runners meet nasty deaths, which I don't find a matter for maudlin tears. As for indulging in moral judgement — King's plan to plant on those Sikhs, I mean—I'm in no position whatever to do so since I've now joined a sort of Mafia myself.'

'You see us like that?'

'I'm afraid I still do. But I told you I'm going to come in and I meant it. You haven't asked why and I thank you for that. Nor do I intend to tell you. Next item on the agenda, please.'

'As the chairman directs.' Sir William chuckled. Some of his normal bounce had returned. He said firmly: 'The next item is that wretched Sen.'

'No, not at all. The next item is you.'

'I don't think I follow.'

'I explained it to your daughter once. Whoever is at the top of this ring must be a pretty big man, we're agreed on that, and you can't expect Big Boy to sit on his bottom while you pick off his satellites one by one. It's his turn to take some action. I think he will.'

'Have a go at me?'

'Or maybe King.'

'King can look after himself. I carry a gun. I've been shot at twice, as I think you know.'

'Can you use it?'

'I'll show you that, but after dinner. Let's go upstairs and see what there is.'

Hanging over the dining room fireplace was the portrait of a handsome woman. Fenwick caught Russell's glance and smiled. 'Penny's mother,' he said. 'I'd like to marry her.'

'What's going to stop you?'

'She is—she won't. And I can't say I entirely blame her. We've lived as we do for years and it's worked. There's a flat in Maida Vale which I pay for, but she has money enough for independence. In fact she's a doctor—rather a good one. She doesn't want to marry me; she doesn't want to marry any man.'

'She sounds a remarkable woman.'

'She is. If I'd met her before I actually did we might both have had a different life. As it is I think she's probably right to let things run on, on a track we're both used to.'

They finished their dinner and Fenwick poured brandy. 'We were talking about guns.'

'So were were.'

'Come up to the gunroom—I'd like to show you.'

Charles Russell was a little surprised. The word 'gunroom' had a special flavour, huge country houses and rich men in tweeds, the insensate slaughter of harmless animals. In this solid Edwardian Wimbledon villa a gunroom sounded distinctly improbable. Fenwick saw Russell's surprise and laughed. 'It's not just a place where I keep a few guns, and if you're wondering what I shoot, I'll show you.'

They went up to the top of the house in a lift and Fenwick unlocked a door with care. He reached inside and turned on a light. 'After you,' he said to Russell politely.

The gallery ran the length of the house, the far wall buttressed by layers of sandbags. 'All inspected by friends,' Fenwick said, 'and passed.'

'But authorized?' Russell inquired.

'Don't be silly.'

Fenwick opened a cupboard and beckoned to Russell. Above were two pairs of expensive guns and a stalking rifle with sight dismounted, the normal armoury of the well-to-do sportsman. But below were two drawers and these were not normal. They held at least a dozen handguns and all of them were in first class conditon. 'Which would you like to try?' Fenwick asked.

'I'd prefer to watch you.'

'Just as you please.'

He chose a marksman's Two-Two and loaded it expertly, then crossed to a row of switches on the wall. He threw one and lights flooded the sandbags.

'You don't use a target?' Russell was curious.

'Oh yes I do—I do indeed.' He pressed another switch and Russell froze. Very slowly, swinging down from the ceiling, appeared the portrait of another woman. She was dressed in an evening gown, wore her jewellery, and her expression was one of patrician disdain. Except that it wasn't patrician: that was spurious. The painter had caught the nuance perfectly, the pretence of breeding hiding the commonplace. And Lady Fenwick must have been stupid too, stupid and extremely insensitive, for no woman with a grain of perception could have failed to feel the painter's contempt for her. She'd have thrown it back in his face, not hung it, especially not in a drawing room where she entertained her woman friends. For that was where she had chosen to put it before Fenwick had moved it up to this gallery. And he'd made one rather startling change to it. Where the woman's heart had been there was nothing: the canvas had been cut away in an oblong of five inches by four. Willy Fenwick pressed a third switch deliberately and a rod rose up from the floor to the vertical. At the top was a frame of thick white paper which measured five by four exactly. It came to rest where the woman's heart had been.

Russell heard Fenwick laugh again. 'A psychiatrist would have very rude words for me. I don't care a damn for that. This does me good. I feel better every time I do it, and better in my case means simply less bitter.' He raised the Two-Two and fired six times smoothly. In the thick white paper were six neat holes.

. . . He may look better but he's still mad as a coot.

'Pretty good shooting,' Charles Russell said blandly.

'Would you care to try yourself?'

'No thank you.'

'A more orthodox target?'

'I'm not in your class.'

'With the rifle, then?'

'I'm out of practice. By the way, is that the gun you carry?'

'Good heavens no, I carry a stopper. A forty-five as it happens—it stops a train. I keep it in the study handy. Let's go there now and have a drink.'

They had their drink but Fenwick seemed restless. Charles Russell said with a hint of acidity:

'I thought you said that foolery did you good. But you're prowling about like a randy tomcat.'

'It's something you said before we ate, that the next move might be theirs—against us. Myself or King to be tiresomely accurate.'

'And you said you could both look after yourselves. Then you took me upstairs to prove you could, and as far as I'm concerned you succeeded.'

'But there's a third you didn't mention. My daughter.'

'What makes you think of her so suddenly?'

'Because she rings every Tuesday at nine o'clock and at this moment it's nearly a quarter past ten. It's a long-standing drill and she's properly dutiful.'

'I can think of a dozen explanations.'

'Of course you can and so can I, but I can also think of one which troubles me.'

'And Penny lives alone?'

'She does for the moment. Like her mother, thank God, she likes a man around, but like her mother again she's hard to please. I think I'm going to ring and check.'

He did so and returned to Russell. 'It rings out,' he said, 'and there isn't an answer.' He wasn't restless now; he was scared. 'I'm going down to Weybridge at once.'

'I'll come with you.'

'It'd save a good deal of time if you did. I've never learnt to drive a car and the driver doesn't sleep in the house. It'd take half an hour at least to get him.'

'But I'm not going to drive that Rolls of yours. My own car's outside so we'll go in that.'

They rose and as they put on overcoats:

'What's the fastest way to Weybridge from here?'

'Up to the top of the Common, then left. Straight down the A3 as far as Esher, then right along Three-One-Seven. A beast.'

They climbed into Russell's car and started. He had

recently sold his venerable Bentley which had been crippling him in repairs and petrol, buying the diametrically opposite, an Italian Thirteen Hundred, hotted up. In the Bentley you'd only changed gear on sharp corners but in this buzz-box you had to change all the time, and if you didn't keep the revs up high you were as likely as not to stall the engine. The car was more than a change in techniques of driving: Russell thought of it as a change in philosophy. Nor did he think his choice a folly. He welcomed any innovation since it helped to keep him young at heart. As they turned into the A3 he asked:

'How long, going briskly?'

'Depends on the traffic. The big stuff uses this road at night but really big stuff is considerately driven. It's the builder's trucks which drive like pigs but the cowboys will be mostly in bed.'

They were in a fast stretch now and Russell was using it. He spoke but he didn't turn his head.

'I saw you bring your gun.'

'I did.'

'Don't use it unless you have to.'

'I won't.'

Near Esher they turned right and Fenwick guided. There was still a certain amount of traffic, mostly private cars returning from parties. It wasn't a stream in which to take chances. Willy Fenwick looked at his watch and frowned.

'We're losing time that may be important.'

Charles Russell didn't answer. He drove.

3

Meaney and Connor were working for money. Acting on Manerji's imperative orders, Sen had found them in a pub in north London where he'd heard that venal Irishmen gathered. They weren't high in their murderous organization, and their duty had been to inform their superiors who would consider the whole project carefully and decide if it was really worth while. But this they had not done for good reason since they knew what the answer would be. That was No. To begin with, Meaney's and Connor's superiors were men of an undoubted experience and this plan had come from a man called Sen. The slightest hint of any Indian connection would have had them shying away like nervous mules.

And secondly, the scheme itself wasn't one of which these men would approve . . . So this Indian wanted to block Sir William by seizing his only daughter and holding her? But that didn't advance the Cause in the least. It wouldn't lower his hardline political profile nor affect his potential for protestant mischief. Ransom? But that, too, was irrelevant. After that job they'd pulled in Worthing they had presently all the money they needed. In any case this was work for professionals, which Meaney and Connor clearly were not. So forget it and go back to your jobs. If we ever need you we'll let you know.

So they were on their own and in it, like others richer, for money. Sen had paid them the first thousand as promised and the rest was due when the job was done. Neither man had trusted Sen but both had needed two thousand badly.

And Connor had an additional worry, one which he couldn't share with Meaney. For the worry was Meaney himself; he was fickle. Connor was much the better educated and his private opinion of Terence Meaney was that he was a crude and unreliable peasant. A huge bear of a man with a winter bear's temper, he had the stage Irishman's taste for excessive liquor, and when he had taken drink he did foolish things. Nevertheless they had to try it. They had a thousand already, were on to another, and that was more than they'd ever saved in years.

A more sophisticated plan than theirs might very well have fallen down, but neither had the experience to risk the perils of anything over-complicated. Meaney had an aunt in north London who would take in Penny Maxim and hide her; she would, that is, for appropriate payment. As for the Weybridge flat, they had cased it. It was a ground floor flat and that made it easier. They'd go in the evening and knock on the door. If that didn't open they'd smash a window. The woman might dial the police but that took time. They wouldn't take guns since they didn't have them. They didn't know that Lesley King had been invited to share Penny Maxim's supper. She was more worried about her father's health than was apparent from her casual manner and her relationship with Lesley was easy. She wanted someone to talk it over with and King's opinion would be well worth having. Charles Russell's would no doubt be better but she'd given Charles Russell a lead and he'd let it pass.

Meaney and Connor stole a car.

Penny Maxim had a job at Heathrow and had been summoned unexpectedly to take another girl's place on the evening shift. So Lesley King had assumed his hostess's duties. He was a good plain cook who enjoyed his cooking and he had prepared a simple meal of roast chicken, bread sauce and new potatoes. When she came in she called out to him gaily, 'I'm as hungry as a horse, but dirty.' She knew better than to peep in the kitchen. Two cooks in a single kitchen was hell. 'But I ought to ring my father first.'

'Bend the rule for once, the bird will spoil.'

'Okay. I'll be out in two minutes.' She was. King had served up and was carving neatly.

'Goodness, that looks good,' she said.

'It ought to be, I took some trouble. No good doing a thing if you don't do it proper.' Occasionally, but only occasionally, he used an adjective instead of an adverb. Penny had never quite decided whether this was an unconscious slip or a deliberate and blackish irony.

They ate the chicken and lit cigarettes. Neither ate more

than one dish at a time.

'I'm horribly late for ringing father.'

He looked at his watch. 'You are that. Go ahead.'

She started to walk to the telephone but stopped at a knock on the door. 'Now at this time of night who the hell could that be?'

'Some collector, I expect—for charity. They're as merciless as duns, often more so.' He was thinking but didn't put it in words that many of them were also misguided, quite apart from those who deducted commission. 'I'll get it,' he said.

He opened the door.

The last thing either man had thought of was to be confronted by another male. Instinctively Connor began to apologize, something about a mistaken number, but Meaney neither spoke nor hesitated. He was standing behind Connor and pushed him; he pushed him powerfully against Lesley King. Off balance, King gave a couple of paces and instantly Meaney was on him himself. King had the ex-policeman's knowledge of the rudiments of self-defence but against the enormous Meaney had little chance. He got an armlock on Meaney but Meaney broke it, as easily as a man with a child. Then he gathered up the still fighting King in a brutal and unbreakable bear hug, while Connor ran behind and clubbed him. Meaney let go and King fell down. Penny had started to move to the telephone and had dialled her first Nine when Connor caught her. He was gentler than Meaney but not very much. He threw Penny into her own armchair. She was looking at King on the floor.

'Don't move.'

Connor sat down and Meaney joined him. He was powerful but badly out of condition and was breathing much more heavily than his scuffle with Lesley King had warranted.

He said to Connor: 'I need a drink.' There was drink on the sideboard and Meaney had noticed it.

Connor hesitated; he didn't like it. Meaney drank far too much and too quickly, but there was drink within sight and Meaney would take it whatever objection Connor raised. He said at last with a clear reluctance:

'Just one, and ten minutes to get your breath back. I'll keep an eye on the girl. And go easy.'

Somewhere on the Three-One-Seven, a little west of deplorable Hersham, Russell asked Fenwick: 'How much longer?' He had caught Fenwick's increasing anxiety and was driving the little car near its limit.

'Ten minutes if we go like this but we've lost a lot of time already. Can't you push her a bit?'

'I dare say I could. But if I do we may not get there at all.'

'I'm inclined to take the risk.'

'You're the boss.'

Russell changed down for a difficult bend and went into it praying she wouldn't break. The engine had begun to scream.

And Connor was sitting trying not to, for he could see that his given ten minutes were far too much. Meaney was drinking whisky straight, three or four fingers, and gulping it greedily. When he had finished his third Connor rose.

'It's time to get the girl away.'

'No.' Meaney looked at a clock. 'You gave me ten minutes and there's two of them left.'

He moved towards the sideboard with his glass.

In the courtyard of Penny's block of flats Russell and Willy Fenwick braked. There were other cars parked but they told them nothing. Both of them ran to Penny's flat, Fenwick perhaps a little heavily, but Russell with surprising agility. Fenwick said: 'I've got a key.'

'But don't go in drawn.'

'Why ever not?'

'Because you'll look the fool of all time if she's sitting there quietly eating her supper.'

'You still think that might be happening?'

'Might.'

'I've never liked looking a fool. You're right.' He gave Russell the key. 'You use it and push the door wide open. I'll go in first—keep behind me.' He was very much the man in command. 'And if I *do* draw keep out of the line of fire.'

Russell said mildly: 'Permission to speak, sir?'

'Granted, but don't waste time.'

'I'm not. Where do you keep that cannon of yours?'

'Shoulder holster.'

'Then kindly pull—I'd like to see it.'

'That sounds reasonable.' Fenwick drew. One moment there wasn't a gun in sight, the next it was covering Russell's stomach.

'Very good,' Russell said. 'Now please put it back.' He took the key. 'Are you ready?'

'Go.'

Russell threw the door open against the stop. Fenwick went in first very quickly. Charles Russell followed and stood to one side. Again the forty-five was out and Russell nodded in quiet approval. Two men had been sitting in chairs but had risen. The gun wasn't pointing at either man but midway between them. It didn't waver. It had a small but very efficient silencer.

. . . My old friend Willy knows his business.

A man was on the floor unconscious and Penny was in a chair, white and tense. Penny said: 'Father!'

'Did they hurt you at all?' The gun-arm had stiffened.

'They didn't hurt me, but they knocked out Lesley.'

Without moving his eyes Willy Fenwick told Russell:

'Take a look at him, please.'

Charles Russell did so. 'Nothing broken but concussed pretty badly. Better leave him as he lies for a bit. You can do a lot of damage. . . .'

'I know.' Fenwick switched to the two standing men. 'Sit down.'

'They hesitated.

'Sit down.'

They sat down. Charles Russell found two other chairs, slipping one under Fenwick neatly. Fenwick's aim didn't change as he settled down in it. Russell took the other beside him. Fenwick inquired of his daughter: 'Okay?'

'I can hold for a bit if that's what you mean.'

'Good girl—keep it cool. We'll do the talking.' He looked at Connor. 'And who are you?'

Connor stared at him; he didn't answer. Fenwick asked Penny: 'You know these men?'

'Never seen them in my life before.'

'Not very helpful.' Sir William reflected. Finally he said to Russell: 'That other one has taken drink.'

'So I had observed myself.'

'You think that might be useful?'

'Possibly.'

'You were an interrogator once. Interrogate.'

'Just as you please.' Russell turned to Meaney. 'Who are you and why are you here?'

Meaney started to speak but Connor silenced him.

Charles Russell reflected in turn, rubbed his chin. At length he said to Fenwick: 'Wing him.'

'But I don't think you understand, dear Charles. When I was showing off in that gallery I was using a target Two-Two—a toy. I could shoot this oaf through the calf with that or any other organ you fancy and it would hurt quite a bit and maybe break him. But I can't do that with what I'm holding. You were rude enough to call it a cannon, and there's something else I didn't tell you. The rounds have been cut—you understand? If I shoot him in the leg with this he won't have very much leg left to stand on. He'll be a cripple for life and ourselves in trouble.'

'Very awkward,' Russell said.

'Indeed.'

These exchanges had not been rehearsed between them and were all the more effective for that. Meaney's fat face was grey and drawn and Connor had begun to fidget. He knew that Meaney was near to breaking. Russell turned to Penny Maxim:

'Give him another drink.'

'You bastard.' It was Connor now.

'Perhaps.' Charles Russell spoke again to Penny. 'Listen carefully to how you do it. You're never to go anywhere near him. Get another glass from the sideboard and fill it, then leave it on the floor beside him. Do it from behind his chair and don't cross your father's line of fire. Understand that?'

'Of course I do.'

She did it neatly.

Lesley King had begun to move and mutter and Charles Russell rose and felt him again. 'I think he's all right. Just leave him a little longer.'

'Right.'

Russell went back to watching Meaney. He had begun to tremble, the spasms increasing. Connor said to him:

'Take that drink and you're dead.'

'But I need a drink.' He sounded like a frustrated child.

'If you talk I'll get you sooner or later.'

'Alternatively,' Russell said softly, 'my friend can get you here and now.' His cool voice changed suddenly, sharp and incisive. 'I'm going to count up to ten.' He began to.

At seven Terence Meaney broke. He picked up the whisky and started to gulp it. Connor rose with a curse and Fenwick fired instantly. The bullet missed Connor's nose by an inch and plaster fell out of the wall in a shower.

'Now you can see what I mean about cutting the bullets.' Connor sat down with another oath, and Meaney's tremble was now the violent shakes. 'I'll tell you, sirs,' he said at last.

'Keep out of this,' Willie Fenwick told Connor.

'What was the plan?' It was now Charles Russell.

'We were going to take the woman.'

'Yes? And acting under whose instructions?'

'Nobody's. We were acting alone.'

'I don't believe you.' Charles Russell considered again, spoke to Fenwick. 'I'm very much afraid we must risk it—risk a serious wound, I mean.'

'Where would you prefer?'

'Where it hurts.'

Fenwick took careful aim but Connor spoke. He looked at Meaney with bitter contempt. 'He's a drunken sot, but I won't have him maimed. We had no orders from our organization. We were working for ourselves. For money.'

'Whose money?'

'An Indian's.'

'What was his name?'

Ten seconds of silence. The gun had come up again.

'Could it be Sen?'

'It was something like that.'

'So Sen wanted a weapon to use against Fenwick here. Do you know why he wanted that?'

'Not really.'

'What do you mean—"*Not really*"?'

'Not properly. But we guessed your friend had been leaning on Sen and Sen wanted the pressure off him. That's all.'

Lesley King had begun to get up unsteadily. 'You can help him now,' Russell said to Penny.

Sir William looked at Charles Russell. 'What now?'

'Nothing else but to let them go.'

'You mean it?'

'What else can we do except call the police, and that would be an utter folly. The police would no doubt be delighted to have them, but what is going to be our story? Invent one which covers what's happened tonight and at the same time doesn't compromise us? You're cleverer than I if you can.'

'I take the point.' Willy Fenwick laughed. 'And they talk

about the luck of the Irish.' He stopped laughing and turned to the two frightened men. 'Get out of here and get out fast. You're now much too hot to be useful in England, so go back to where you came from and rot there.'

'I mean to,' Connor said.

'That's wise.'

When the men had gone Charles Russell took over again. 'There's no point in talking tonight, we're all tired.'

'You don't think they'll come back?'

'Most unlikely.'

'I'd be happier to have a man here.' Penny's words were ambiguous: Russell sensed they were meant to be. He turned his head to look at Penny. If she were looking at King....

She was looking at Russell.

King said to Fenwick: 'I'll take the gun.'

'Don't be silly, Lesley. You've taken a beating.'

'Then I'll stay.' It was Fenwick.

Russell said quietly: 'He's *your* man, Willy, not mine. You owe it to him to see him home.'

'You sound a trifle feudal.'

'I am.' Russell held out his hand. 'The gun, if I may borrow it. I may not be an artist like you, but I do know how to use it still.'

When the others had gone, Penny Maxim laughed. 'I called you a coolie once. You are.'

'And the comment which followed?' He hadn't forgotten.

'Need I repeat it?'

'No you need not.' Meaney had left them a little whisky. 'May I mix us a drink?'

She made a mock curtsy. 'All is yours.'

'Including a razor to use in the morning?'

'I've a razor and pyjamas too.'

4

Russell had been sincerely convinced that this was a battle of strike and counter-strike, but the next move came from neither combatant but from the old gods who punished human *hubris*.

For Sen had woken that morning uneasily, hoping that all would go well but fearing it wouldn't. He knew it was a local axiom never to get mixed up with Indians, and for the Irish he had a similar instinct. You simply couldn't rely on their word, far less on any practical competence. Men like those two in the pub. . . . He shivered. But he'd been given his outrageous orders and these two had been all he'd been able to find.

Sen had gone off to his work and was worrying when the house phone rang on his desk unexpectedly.

'The Inspector would like to see you, sir.'

'Now?' Sen was a little surprised. The Inspector was one of those travelling mandarins whom most Foreign Services kept on their books, and his business was to tour the posts, reporting on their state of efficiency and if possible cutting down their costs. He couldn't give orders but could have orders issued, and such instructions very often stuck. Sen had talked to him twice already and the Inspector had seemed reasonably satisfied. Or had given that impression. He was an Indian.

Sen took the lift upstairs and knocked on the Inspector's door. A voice said: 'Come in,' and V. S. Sen did so.

'Good morning, Mr Sen.'

'Good morning.'

The Inspector hadn't got up for the greetings. He was a Sindhi whose father had lost his home when all Sindh had gone to Pakistan. He was thin and sharp featured, the typical Amil, as dangerous as an angry cobra.

'I want to talk about this posting of yours, the one back to India and the Foreign Ministry. You're very lucky to get it, you know.'

That wasn't Sen's own opinion at all. He'd been an efficient official; he thought he'd earned it.

'Naturally there'll be certain formalities.'

'The period when my successor takes over?'

'There'll be that, of course. There is also another.' The Inspector bent his thin shoulders forward. 'The allowances in this post are fair and you're not noted for keeping open house. Naturally you will have saved some money.'

Sen sucked his breath in, then let it out. The tooth on his lip was showing once more. He knew exactly what was coming next, for this was the way his country was run.

'They're adequate but a man can't save on them.'

'Then how have you sent money home? Much more than your family need to keep them.'

It would have been pointless to ask how he knew. Sen waited.

'Quite substantial sums and all used wisely. And no doubt you have a balance here still. The Party would never be unmindful if you showed your appreciation properly.'

'I have nothing,' Sen said. It was true. A few days ago he'd owned two thousand, but he'd parted with one of those to those horrible men. As for the other he'd made a promise to pay it. Not that he felt obliged to keep it, but technically there existed a debt. It was therefore technically true he had nothing.

'I believe you have a thousand pounds. Never mind how I know but I do. You bank at an Indian bank, you see.'

'I have a debt to pay and then I'll have nothing.'

The Sindhi had begun to lose patience, panting a little and wiping his forehead. 'You have a posting—as I said, a lucky one. But no posting in any service is watertight. I have only to make a report. . . .'

He showed most of his teeth, but whether it was a smile or a snarl V. S. Sen was a little uncertain. In any case it wasn't relevant for the threat was sufficiently firmly based. An adverse report wouldn't take him to Delhi; it would take him to some dreary black stateling where he'd rot for the next four years at least. Sen knew when he was beaten, said;

'I'll write you a cheque to the Party's Treasurer.'

'My friend, you will do no such thing. You will bring me the money here in cash.'

Sen was down but he wasn't quite out. With a sudden flare of defiance he said:

'I won't do that.'

'But I think you will.' The Inspector was suddenly almost friendly and a friendly Sindhi made V. S. Sen shiver. 'You can't really think I know nothing about it.'

'Know about what?'

'How you made that money.'

Sen started to get up, sat down again. The Sindhi went on with a cold smooth menace. 'I can see your mind working, my friend, so I'll read it. If I know about this, if I've turned a blind eye to it, then of course I'm covering up a drug traffic. Which might give you some counterhold on me. Yes? But it doesn't, you see, for I'm not just conniving, There's no harm in telling you now since you're helpless. I'm as deep in this as you are—in my own way. When I discovered how you were making money I naturally went to the man who pays you. What else could a poor man do?' He grimaced. 'I get five per cent on whatever comes over, whereas you, I believe, get ten or fifteen. I don't think that a fair division, and I don't think a thousand excessive to even it.' He leant forward again; he had poisonous breath. 'So bring me that thousand here in tenners. Get it before your bank shuts. Go.'

And get it, the other privately thought, before I myself collapse disgracefully. He went back to his room and did collapse but he pulled himself together finally. He sent for a taxi and went to his bank. There was only one thing he could do and he did it.

He asked for a thousand pounds in tenners.

Meaney and Connor were driving home. Meaney had a

flask and was using it. 'I didn't like it a bit,' he said uneasily, 'That man we had to cosh. He was fuzz.'

Connor nodded. 'Policeman or ex-policeman—yes. By now I can smell them a mile away. He came to before the other two threw us out. That's bad because he'll have seen our faces.'

'Boy friend perhaps,' Meaney said unhopefully. He sounded disapproving. He drank too much, he was dirty and smelt, but in matters of sex he was unforgiving.

'Then what about the other two? What made them arrive when they did?'

'I don't know.'

'I don't like the look of it either,' Connor said. 'Somebody must have grassed. But who?'

'Could that Wog have grassed himself?'

'Why should he?'

'If he was in with the police to lay a trap.'

'Then why did they let us go?'

'I don't know.'

There was a silence while they thought it over. Finally Connor said with decision:

'This is getting us no place. The fact is that that copper saw us, and two other men to make it worse. We've got to have money to get away quick. Lie low for a bit at home. Just like the man said. But that's expensive.' He looked at Meaney with something like hatred. 'That game was as crooked as hell,' he said. 'You'd have spotted it if you hadn't been sozzled. A thousand pounds down the drain in an evening.'

'That Wog still owes us another thousand.'

'But we didn't get the girl.'

'What of it? How is he going to check that we didn't? I mean if we go right away. Tonight.'

'For once you've had a good idea.'

Connor stopped at a phone box and used it briskly. The thing if done at all must be done at once. He rang up V.S. Sen in his bed.

'Mr Sen?'
'Who is it?'
'You owe us a thousand. We're coming to get it.'
'But gentlemen, sirs. . . .'
'We're coming now.'

Sen was mentally shattered, his thinking in chaos. His emotions chased each other around, fear, horror, disgust, then always fear again; above all the sense that it wasn't fair, the feeling of all clever men in adversity that fate had played them a dirty trick.

For he'd deserved that posting, he really had. He'd worked hard and well and, more important, had made no mistake of any kind. Handling drugs? But that didn't count. He'd made a good deal of money doing so, but that money had not been bribes; far from it. He'd sold no favours to any fellow Indian, nor withheld from another the services due to him. If Europeans got hooked on drugs and destroyed themselves that was nothing to trouble an Indian conscience.

So he'd honestly earned his posting home. He hadn't seen his wife for years, not since they'd given him three months' leave and an air passage. The children would be almost unrecognizable. Delhi wasn't Bengal but at least it was India. He could motor east and visit his land, the fields which his earnings had saved and revitalized. By now, no longer crippled by debt, they were a patrimony any man could be proud of. He thought of the sluggish, slow-moving waters choked by weed which, when it flowered, was beautiful. South Africa had banned it. Materialists.

A beautiful country then, the best on earth. And now that cunning Sindhi pig had robbed him of any present hope of it. He had taken his last thousand pounds, and that thousand pounds, as matters had gone, was his only defence against men who terrified him. He had never been struck in his life—no, never. Not even by his mother or ayah. Upper-class Indian women never did. Servants wouldn't have dared to dream of it.

But those Irishmen would do more than strike. They would cause him great pain and he couldn't take it; he'd give in to their demands at once. But that was the horror, the final fear. For he couldn't give in, he hadn't the means to. Like a man being tortured to give up a secret and the man didn't have it to give his tormentors. They'd go on and on and on. . . .

But there was one thing he could do and he did it. He rang up the police and asked for protection.

The station sergeant was middle-aged and experienced; he had been asked for this before and knew the drill. Mostly such requests came from lunatics, from people incorrectly convinced that some person or persons unknown were after them, and even if the request sounded reasonable it was one of the trickiest traps in the book. It could be authorized only by senior officers and the sergeant was a long way from that. It was also four in the morning. He wanted his bed.

'I'm afraid we're very short-handed, sir.'

'But I tell you, they're going to injure me terribly.'

The voice was foreign and the sergeant suspicious. These demands for protection were bad enough, but when they came from foreigners the dangers progressed algebraically. One didn't want to mix oneself up in some inter-racial brawl or vendetta. And the caller had said his name was Sen. That sounded Indian, and on that he had had a specific warning.

The sergeant had five minutes to spare; he was a kindly man and he went on soothingly:

'Do you know these men's names, sir?'

'Meaney and Connor.'

For the first time the sergeant was mildly interested. Irish, he thought—there might really *be* something. He made a quick note.

'Do you know where they live?'

'Not their addresses but they've talked of north London.

That's where they have what they called their pads. I think that means their lodgings.'

'It does.' The sergeant's voice was not ironical for he wasn't an ironical man. North London was full of immigrant Irish but he made another deliberate note. 'And your own address, sir?'

Sen gave his address and the sergeant recorded it. At least any note he left would be accurate.

'May I ask your profession?'

Sen hesitated but finally gave it. 'I'm an Attaché in the Indian High Commission.'

Instantly the sergeant froze. His manor held more than a single diplomat and his instructions on how to deal with them were precise and also entirely mandatory. You fended them off with the longest pole handy and you never made the smallest commitment. Then you wrote it down for a senior officer. The sergeant said:

'Then I think that's all, sir.'

'But I'm in danger, I tell you.'

'We'll do what we can.'

'You must give me protection. I'm entitled to that.'

'Do you realize what police protection means?' The sergeant wasn't soothing now, he was wary and more than a little irritated. 'It means two men at least on eight hour shifts. We don't have that sort of manpower available.' He might have added but was too wise to do so: 'In affairs which as often as not are mares' nests.'

'Please,' Sen said. 'Do something. Please.' He had started to weep and the sergeant heard him. It confirmed what he had decided already—that the farther he kept out of this the better.

'We'll do what we can, sir,' he said again.

He rang off and completed his careful note. . . . Those diplomats were hell to deal with. One minute they'd ask outrageous favours and the next, if you sent a man on inquiries, they'd be complaining to the Whitehall brass that you'd been violating their preposterous privileges.

Sen looked at the telephone dead in his hand, then replaced it and sat down, still weeping. Another man might have made for the bottle but V. S. Sen only drank when obliged to. Alcohol was one of those western vices, socially acceptable but nevertheless entirely degrading. Instead he made for his radio-gramophone, choosing a record of classical sitar. It soothed him as it frayed most westerners, the endless wobbling round a handful of notes, the total lack of definition. It went on for ever, like reincarnation, like his own life would be when they'd finally killed him. He was much less afraid of death than of pain.

The telephone on his desk rang sharply.

He rose and answered it almost eagerly. Perhaps they weren't coming — just threats on the telephone. Perhaps he could talk them off. Perhaps . . .

It was the Night Officer from the High Commission. A despatch had come in and been duly decoded. The Duty Officer thought it important. Mr Sen should come to the office at once.

'Read it over,' he said instead.

'I cannot.' The voice was shocked to the point of scandal. 'It came in code and this line's an open one.'

'Then have it sent round.'

'The night messenger, sir, is sick, sir. I . . .'

'Then bring it round yourself.'

'But sir . . .'

Sen rang off before the protests swamped him. He knew perfectly well that the Duty Officer was not supposed to leave the building. So he'd stick to the rules and stay where he was, or conceivably he'd obey Sen's order. In which case there'd be at least a witness.

He went back to his chair and the twanging sitar. The supporting drummer banged dithyrambically, seldom quite on the beat and quite inescapable. V. S. Sen let his breath out contentedly. It was the music of total despair. He despaired.

When the knock came on the door he opened it. If he

didn't they'd find means to do so. What was the point in resisting stupidly? The police had refused him immediate help and he didn't spring from a fighting people. His tongue and his brains were his weapons.

Useless. Useless when all you could tell was the truth and you knew in advance that the truth would be laughed at.

Meaney and Connor came in quickly and Meaney shut the door behind him. Connor wasted no time in approaches.

'We've come for our money. A thousand pounds.'

'So you got the woman?'

'Of course we did.'

'Where are you keeping her?'

'We'll tell you when you've paid us our money.'

'The second thousand I promised to pay you?' Sen had decided his line already since in practice he didn't have an alternative; he wasn't going to prevaricate. Instead he'd tell the truth but not hopefully. 'I don't deny the debt,' he said.

'That's something.'

'But I can't pay it, or not at this moment. I had an emergency and had to meet it.'

'Did you indeed?' It was Connor, reflective. Meaney simply said:

'You bastard.'

'Be quiet.' Connor was undecided, thinking. He knew more of the world than Meaney did and he could guess at the sort of sudden emergency which could strike at a man in Sen's position. Some woman, he thought, or even blackmail.

But he looked round the room; it was comfortably furnished. Not luxuriously but there was a hi-fi and a rather expensive one. 'Your lot always has money,' he said at last.

'Now I've only my pay.'

'I don't believe you.'

'I'll give you a hundred a week till the debt is settled.' It was the sum he was saving by working for Manerji.

'A promise on a promise. No go.' Connor signalled to

Meaney; he had made up his mind. 'You can start on him,' he said.

Meaney did so. He hit Sen in his pot stomach and dropped him. Sen lay on the floor and fought for breath. Connor stood over him.

'Well?'

'No money.'

Connor said to Meaney: 'The boot,' then after a minute: 'That's enough.'

Sen hadn't tried to get up. He lay there groaning, passively taking it. He hadn't begged for mercy; he took the punishment. Connor knelt down, put his face near Sen's.

'Well?' he asked again.

'No money.' The words were audible but only just.

Meaney suddenly lost his wicked temper. He'd been kicking at the ribs and getting them, now he aimed for the head and got that too. Sen stiffened and tried to rise, fell back. Meaney was berserk, he kicked twice more.

'Jesus,' Connor said; he knelt down again. He felt for Sen's pulse but couldn't find it. He opened his shirt, put his ear to his heart. When he got up his face was frozen.

'You bloody fool,' he said. 'You've killed him.'

As they went down the stairs another man passed them. He was an Indian carrying an emblazoned despatch box.

5

They met at Fenwick's house at noon. Lesley King had had a good night's rest and an X-ray had revealed no damage. Penny was rather quiet, Fenwick jubilant.

Charles Russell sat a little withdrawn, listening to the talk as it flowed. They were talking about the drug traffic ladder, repeating what he had heard before. Above the pushers were the men who distributed from the man who had handled the latest consignment, and at the top of the pile was the hated master. That had been Lesley King's premise, one made from a professional experience, and they hadn't done so badly so far. Not at all. They had fixed the two runners, or King would have fixed them if more ruthless and determined rivals hadn't shot his bird under his eager nose.

Moreover the early evening papers had carried Sen's death in banner headlines:

DIPLOMAT FOUND DEAD IN FLAT

Sen had been found by another Indian, also in the High Commission, who'd been carrying an urgent despatch. He hadn't been able to get an answer so had called the porter to open the door for him. Sen had been dead on the floor; he'd been beaten. The police were treating the matter as murder and two men in north London were helping inquiries.

. . . Two men in north London? That must be significant. North London was vague — it was meant to be vague — but two communities had established enclaves there. One was coloured and Russell shook his head. High caste Indians seldom tangled with Blacks. But the other was thickly, triumphantly Irish, and anyone could make a mistake.

It was Russell's experienced guess that Sen had done so. He'd made the worst of all, the big one. He had hired two men of dubious background and then had tried to doublecross them. He had got himself mixed up with the Irish and that was more dangerous than handling heroin.

Russell said suddenly: 'Poor fat bastard.'

The others stared at him, then went back to their theories.

Russell sat in dissenting silence, for events didn't strike him as wholly fruitful. If Big Boy was half as big as Russell guessed, he could replace his lackeys without much difficulty, which would leave them for an indefinite period shooting at rabbits instead of the tiger. The Indian tiger immune in his jungle.

Charles Russell now wanted his skin very badly.

And another aspect had begun to offend him. If he had

had to find a single word for events as they had so far occurred it would have been the simple but damning word 'untidy.' It had been untidy to throw Harry Maxim to death, untidy to try and scare off Russell when he hadn't at that moment been in. The business of the two renegade Sikhs (renegade because Sikhs as a whole were men who wouldn't touch drugs with a pole) had had a certain grim humour but that, too, had been messy. And as for the affair last night. . . .

Charles Russell frowned; he had not been amused. There'd been only one word for that again, and that was the worst word he knew. The whole plan had been deplorably amateur.

Which meant it was time for a hard old pro to put an end to this rather violent incompetence.

He said suddenly: 'We're getting nowhere.'

Fenwick asked sharply: 'You're backing out?'

'No, not at all, I'm in deeper than ever. But the deep end isn't here, it's in India. Isn't that what you want—the man at the top?'

'Of course I do.'

'I doubt if you'll get him by smashing his ladder.'

'Then what do you suggest?'

'Go to India.'

'All of us?'

'No, just me. I've a friend there and he owes me a service.' He was thinking of a man named Venkata, now head of what was called the Bureau.

There was a silence till Fenwick said finally: 'Thank you.'

'When do you plan to go, sir?' It was King.

'Tomorrow on the first flight that'll take me.'

'Then I'll drive you home and help you pack.' Penny Maxim got up as she spoke. She knew the last thing Russell would want would be chatter. He had said he would go and go he would. There was nothing like sharing a bed with a man for learning how his essential mind worked.

She woke him in the small hours, fretting. 'I can't sleep,'

she told him.

'You've a very good reason to.'

'I know but . . . Charles, take care.'

'Take care of what?'

'Yourself of course.'

He said sleepily: 'I'm not a hero, you know. I don't go dashing about into danger.'

'But those motorcyclists, the men at my flat. . . .'

'I've got a powerful friend in India. That's why I'm going.'

In half an hour he was fast asleep again. It would have taken him very much less than that if it hadn't been for another distraction.

But Penny lay awake still thinking. She had good reason to wish Charles Russell safe. And, she thought smiling, maybe two. If she were lucky at last, she'd have two reasons.

THREE

THREE

1

Manerji was more than big enough to have earned himself a public nickname, and behind their hands men called him 'The Man'. By caste he was a moneylender but he'd moved a very long way from that. He owned factories and shipyards and banks; he was one of the last tycoons the Presence had left. Intellectuals were currently running his country and he knew he was both feared and hated. It was illogical since he made much money which they taxed at a rate he considered outrageous, even though he kept two sets of books as Indian business men always had. It was stupid to persecute men who made money but that was the way the new men thought.

And the Presence, he had remembered. Yes indeed. The Presence would like to destroy him finally.

The shadow was there and inescapable but at that moment he'd had a more pressing worry. Hard drugs were also a part of his empire, and he'd been reading a report from his creature Sen, made before that creature had died humiliatingly. When this report had come in he'd been drinking sweet tea—he never drank coffee, nor smoked, nor touched alcohol. One of his secretaries had brought it, decoded. His feet were unshod and he was wearing a dhoti. Manerji wouldn't have servants in trousers.

The Man had read it with a troubled frown, a complication which he didn't welcome. He wasn't actively against the West but coolly indifferent to all it stood for. Clearly it was ripe for collapse, and if it chose to compound what he saw as degeneracy by habits which he considered disgusting that wasn't a matter which touched his ethos.

Especially when those disgusting habits made great profits which he could easily hide.

Manerji employed Sen for drugs but he had more professional contacts for information, journalists and business friends, spies whom he paid in the business friends' offices. He knew most things about young Fenwick and his father. Young Fenwick had been distinctly unfortunate, not in himself but simply to Manerji. For he hadn't been some third-rate student, some dropout riding a spurious thrill; he'd been a steady young man with a solid background and his father was a Member of Parliament, a man with a reputation for toughness. The boy had been his only son and Sir William had taken his death very hard. Manerji knew he had taken it hard. He had even hired an ex-policeman to work for him.

Let him do that if he wished. The ring was sound.

Or so he had thought till this tiresome report. Now it looked as though William Fenwick was dangerous. . . . Some man at V. S. Sen's safe. That was bad. As it happened there'd been a new consignment, which explained why Sen had brought the Sikhs with him. They weren't pushers but higher up the line, the runners to the men who peddled. That suggested information too—the other side also must have its sources. Then the man had been thrown through the window and killed. That was bad again but probably manageable. There'd been an inquest and they'd called Mr. Sen. Manerji despised all diplomats but would employ them for their undoubted advantages. So Sen had done the brass-faced lying and the Sikhs had supported with Sikh stolidity. Nobody else had been present to challenge them.

So far so good but the rest might be ominous . . . . Charles Russell of all people dead or alive.

Manerji had clucked irritably, not at the fact of Russell's involvement but at V. S. Sen's otiose explanation. Who did this man think that Manerji was, some ignorant peasant scratching his fields? For of course he had heard of Colonel Charles Russell. It hadn't been many years ago when Russell had still been officially working, that they'd crossed swords on a very different matter. Russell had won and Manerji feared him.

He reread the decoded report, more relaxed. There was a good deal Manerji resented, the excerpts from books of reference which naturally he already possessed, the speculations about Charles Russell's past when he himself had much more than opinions; but give Sen his due, he'd recorded one fact. Charles Russell was living quite close to Sen so had a legitimate reason to be passing his flat. True that he'd also gone up with the policeman but that only established the sergeant's competence in a matter which Sen's status made delicate.

. . . A diplomat indeed! God help us. But he was useful because he was poor and greedy.

Manerji sent for more tea and drank it. Russell's presence could be explicable but no sensible man would just leave it at that. Charles Russell had lived in a dangerous world, he was formidable and a friend of Fenwick. Fenwick clearly meant mischief and had indeed started it, unless this thief whom they'd interrupted had really been an ordinary thief.

A hypothesis which the Man had discounted.

In life as in business the Man played the percentages and the percentages suggested strongly that Maxim's had not been an ordinary break-in. So Fenwick and this ex-policeman King who had a background as a professional drug hunter had sent Harry Maxim in to get the proof. He had failed and been thrown out of a window, and he'd landed within a foot of Charles Russell.

The percentages again were clear: Russell lived within half a mile of Sen and had been walking along the street quite innocently, but the Man knew more than he liked about Russell. Potentially he was a danger, the biggest. And he had been to call on Maxim's widow. Inquiries had been made about her and she was Fenwick's illegitimate daughter.

The percentages now pointed differently. Russell could still have been passing innocently but his subsequent actions were surely not innocent. Charles Russell had taken a hand. That was ominous.

Manerji had considered carefully before he sent another instruction to Sen. Russell must be somehow neutralized. Murder could still be bought with money and with most men that might well be possible, but Charles Russell wasn't most men—not at all. His death otherwise than in his bed would bring more than one security service buzzing around the body like flies, to say nothing of the English police who were still rather harder to bribe than most. They'd start probing and ferreting, sniffing the trail out, and the Man knew where that trail would lead.

This was urgent and he would have liked to telephone, but he knew that the telephone had been tapped for years. But his code was still safe so he'd answered in that. He had smiled as he wrote his careful instructions. They had a phrase for this in he western world: in England and America they called it putting on the frighteners. That should give Russell pause for thought, and time was of the heart and essence. But Fenwick would need more drastic medicine since Fenwick had the greater motive.

Snatch his daughter and hold her. That should stop him.

The Man had sent his orders to Sen and Sen had died in trying to obey them.

Two miles from where Manerji had sent his signal four men sat round a mahogany table. They had broken his code and were reading the transcript.

They were a curiously assorted quartet, but less so when you considered their object. For this wasn't an official body, it was the creature of an almost allpowerful Presence; and that Presence hated Manerji and everything that Manerji stood for, quite apart from the fact that he still owned power, a commodity which should never be shared.

All four were in a very bad temper for they'd been called before the Presence and tongue-lashed. It had been done in an inimitable style, arrogant and autocratic, but by some miracle stopping just short of plain insult. All of them were men of some standing, and to be spoken to like recalcitrant children had sorely tried their respective patiences. The Kashmiri had dared to answer back.

'You complain of the lack of effective action but you have made that action almost impossible.' He was far from a stooge and the other's caste equal.

'I don't think I understand you, sir.'

'Manerji runs a drug ring in England. We have evidence to break that up, or rather to let the English police break it.' He looked sideways at the Madrassi, who nodded. 'We have excellent police contacts in England and they'd be delighted with the real help we could give them. But I doubt if that course would advance your intention. If the English police take open action, with or without assistance from us, there is still going to be an enormous scandal. There is good evidence, maybe better than good, the Manerji runs the whole thing from India, but dare you bring him before our Courts for drug peddling? There'd be an even more resounding row at a moment when it's very important that the image of this State should be lotus white. What you really want as we understand you is to destroy a man you consider an enemy. Which is something I can understand. But you've told us you will not pay the price of nailing him through a scandal in drugs.'

He was stared at with something quite close to hatred. What he had said had been clear and lucid, and the Presence was more than clever enough to realize that it was perfectly true.

The Presence slid away into irrelevance. 'You're politicians, aren't you? Then act politically.'

So this hand-picked committee sat and deliberated. Its brief had been perfectly clear and simple: they were to get enough on Manerji to break him without appeal, and finally. This they had accepted reluctantly for their brief had been hedged by that crippling proviso: all this must be done without a breath of scandal, especially of international scandal.

The four men frowned over Manerji's message, a Kashmiri, a Muslim, a Madrassi, a Christian. There was an instruction to speak in Hindi if possible but these men were conducting their business in English. There was good and sufficient reason for this, for the man from Madras spoke little Hindi and the Muslim, whose natural tongue was Urdu, declined to speak Hindi as a matter of principle. His presence at all was in fact political, as was that of the fourth man, the Indian Christian. This was supposed to be a secular State, though every non-Hindu knew it wasn't, but the appearance of any religious bias was tabu throughout the whole system's network, right down to a body which didn't exist, or didn't exist in any book.

As any Indian would at once have assumed, the Kashmiri was running the meeting's affairs. He was tall and thin and coldly superior. He looked at the Christian, asked softly but firmly:

'Enough do you think?'

'I hardly think so. It's an instruction to commit a crime, and if we pass it to the English authorities they may or may not be forced to take action. But where will that get us here in India?'

'Not very far,' the Muslim said. He hadn't the others' agile brains but he could take a point when it was banged on his nose.

The chairman nodded and looked down at the table. 'Venkata?' he asked the Madrassi.

He had one of those interminable Madrassi names, six or seven syllables, even ten, but it did begin with Venkata, and that was what he was always called.

The Kashmiri's voice had slightly changed and Venkata, who was sensitive, noticed it. Of the four men present he alone was a policeman and a policeman of a special sort. He was half a generation older than any of the others there and his roots went back to the Imperial Police. He was well into his sixties now but they'd kept him on for his unmatched experience, because he alone in all of India could talk to a senior foreign policeman on anything like equal terms. But the others were men of Hind and he wasn't.

He knew what the others were thinking perfectly. They cared not a damn for Manerji's drug traffic since all of them shared the same opinion, that if Europeans were fools enough to destroy their bodies by taking hard drugs that wasn't a matter to weigh on the conscience of an older and saner civilization. The Madrassi thought this view irresponsible. He'd been a policeman before he'd been given the Bureau and he still thought as he'd been trained to think. The Muslim picked up the decoded signal. 'I don't think this helps us very much. The drug side is there still, the shattering scandal.'

The Christian said: 'But it's common kidnapping. A snatch, I rather think they call it.' He was proud of his colloquial English.

Venkata, the man from the south, said nothing at all; he had nothing to say. He knew that he was odd man out and as an ex-policeman he had different values. The other three were politicians, but Venkata, like Lesley King, had deep and strongly conditioned prejudices. If that, he thought dourly, was what foolish men called them. Any talk of drugs raised his hackles fiercely. He would have blown the whole affair wide open, thinking his day well spent in doing so, if it hadn't been for the other three who were gunning for Manerji, not for his drug traffic. Naturally—they were all in politics. Naturally—they had had their orders. Naturally—they were paid to obey them.

'Then what do we do?' the Muslim asked.

'Nothing,' the chairman said at once, 'or nothing for the immediate moment.' He tapped the decoded instruction firmly. 'Now what have we here?' he asked rhetorically, answering his own question promptly. 'We have an instruction to arrange a kidnapping, the obvious motive to halt Fenwick finally. Quite logical, given the Man's need to do so. But the point is not the instruction to kidnap but the person to whom the instruction goes. Who is a man called Sen in our own Foreign Service. No doubt he is a clever man or he wouldn't be employed by Manerji, but none of us has the slightest reason to suppose he can organize violent crime.' He looked round the table. 'Any comment?'

'I hadn't thought of that,' the Muslim said.

'Then I suggest that we all of us think of it hard. He will try to do as he's told since he must, but the chances that he'll do it successfully are much longer than I'd care to bet on.'

'And so?' someone asked.

'I cannot foresee it. But I'm confident something will go very wrong, and if something goes wrong it could give us an opening.'

'But how do you think Sen's going to handle it?' It was the Christian being Christianly practical. He might have added, but didn't give words to the thought, that he shared the Kashmiri's opinion entirely. Bengalis like Sen were admittedly clever, they were brilliant at any sort of intrigue, but somewhere between the idea and fulfilment something was apt to slip in practice. Or if that didn't happen then the Lord in His Wisdom just arranged for a piece of appalling bad luck. It was fortunate He chose to do so since if He didn't no Christian could live long in India however loudly the rest of them prated of tolerance.

So he asked again: 'How will Sen handle it?'

'I don't know that and I don't pretend to.' It was the high caste Hindu who would seldom commit himself. 'But I can guess where he might look for help.'

'Where's that?'

The chairman said with insulting patience: 'In books you read a good deal of nonsense about people going out to hire hoodlums. I suspect that in practice it isn't so easy.' He looked at the ex-policeman inquiringly. 'Would you confirm that?'

'Yes I would. Unless you're in that world yourself it's quite difficult to hire a good strongarm. But Fenwick is a Member of Parliament who sits for a seat in Northern Ireland and he's what they call a hardline Unionist. We know he's been shot at twice already and it's obvious who did the shooting. There are plenty of those in London, you know, so Sen would have a source to go to.'

'I suppose that's possible,' somebody said.

'Then we'll wait upon events?'

'As we must.'

The Madrassi went back to his modest lodgings and drank a little whisky unhappily. It was difficult to get and expensive but he'd always liked a drink in the evening. He was depressed and he was also frustrated. He knew perfectly what the others thought of him: he was a small stout man with a rather dark skin, a Dravidian from the deepest south with an impossible language which none of them spoke. He had started life as an ordinary constable and won his Commission from British hands. They had kept him on to run the Bureau but in the international league of such Bureaux his own stood very low in the table, not less than ten below Shin Beth and a mile from the two which really counted. He'd been asked to join the three politicians only because of a lifetime's experience, not because he might influence secret policy. So he knew very well what the others thought of him and he suspected they knew what he thought of them. They were politicians, venal time-servers, and if he concealed his contempt he was doing well. Conversely they seldom bothered to hide their own.

He was conscious of an increasing nostalgia. . . . Those had been the golden days—real police work mostly free from corruption. Real Security too, not personal politics. The proudest week in this ageing Madrassi's life was the week when he'd actually worked with Charles Russell.

He looked at what was left of the bottle; he didn't know

where the next was coming from but he decided nevertheless to finish it. He did so, drinking a toast each time. He drank to the old days, to men he'd admired. First of them had been Colonel Charles Russell.

Manerji sat in his fine old house. It rose in the old city proudly, two miles from New Delhi's imperial longueurs and much further than that in thought and tradition. It hadn't been altered in generations for Manerji's forebears had built it well. It stood in one of the very few openings in the labyrinth of narrow streets, its façade on a market with shops each side. The front was of wood with bracketed balconies, the spaces between the shuttered windows elaborately carved and painted. Two studded teak doors gave access to the courtyard. They were fine Burmese teak, not some rubbish from an African jungle. Outside them an ancient doorkeeper idled, half asleep in the stifling heat, chewing betel. The nut had made his teeth as red as the sash he wore across one shoulder. The brass badge on it hadn't been polished for years, but this was a Hindu family house not an office in the slick new capital. Manerji's great-great-grandfather had always kept some form of gatekeeper. It was unthinkable that Manerji shouldn't, though his presence today was entirely pointless.

Manerji sat in a ground floor room which opened on the untidy courtyard—old carts and a tonga with ill-kept ponies, hens scratching in the timeless dust. In the brash new town was a brash new office and a car and a driver to take him in style, but this was where he did his thinking. The floor was of cowdung and Manerji shoeless.

So he sat on a string cot and thought. In a corner was a single carved figure, one of the numerous manifestations of the goddess who was his family's patroness—his family's and therefore his caste's. To Manerji they were barely distinguishable. His people had been village moneylenders since the Aryans came down from the north. Manerji and one or two like him were very much more than that by now, but the instincts of business, of lending and usury, were as strong in their blood as they ever had been. Before the effigy burned a single lamp, a wick floating in an earthenware saucer.

Manerji inclined his head, his hands before his face, palms together. He was going to need the goddess's help. It was killingly hot in the little room for only an old-fashioned punkah stirred the air. In his office he'd put in electric fans, a concession he'd been obliged to make since foreign visitors might simply assume that his business couldn't afford electricity. But even in his modern office he'd declined to instal any air conditioning, believing, as older Indians did, that air conditioning could make a man impotent.

He was normally very hard to ruffle but this morning he was depressed and irritable. More important, he had been warned by his wife, which was something which happened extremely seldom and it was therefore all the more disturbing when the black cloud appeared in a peaceful sky.

She had come into his room uninvited, a liberty she didn't take often, and he noticed at once she was dressed with formality, rings on her toes, her best sari, her bangles. These were in a real sense her war paint; she gave him a formal greeting but didn't sit.

'I think you should be very careful.'

'And why is that?' he asked politely. He was polite because he was rarely otherwise. The marriage had been arranged but it worked. She had brought him a considerable dowry and her family's money was meshed with his own. She was as shrewd in her way as he was himself and he trusted her all the way. He had to.

So he repeated politely: 'Why is that?'

'You know the Presence would like to break you.'

'Of course I know that. I have known it for years.'

'Four men have been named to bring it about.'

'Where did you hear that?'

'Other women.'

How they chattered, he thought. But he'd known that

too. He moved his head, not a nod, not a shake, the characteristic Indian woggle, watching her as he did so reflectively. She had borne him five children, four sons and one daughter, and that was a fine economical record. It was a pity that in doing so she had given him only fleeting pleasure but he didn't resent what he knew was inevitable. In his wife's world you broke the rules at your peril. Ladies Didn't Move; that was final, and Manerji's wife was extremely conventional.

'I will bear what you say in mind.'

'You'd be wise to.'

He had returned to his communion with the goddess, still ruffled. The only visitor at his home that morning was an Englishman, retired from the Indian Civil Service, now settled in India, ageing rapidly. Manerji had nothing against him except that he'd chosen to stay in India. This he considered a loss of caste. His Service had been the lords and masters, appointed by a British Minister and owing their allegiance to London. When this ended as it was bound to end—Manerji had a Hindu's timescale which was very little short of infinity—when this finished with an undignified whimper it was shameful to stay on subservient. He would never have done such a thing himself and had nothing but a concealed contempt for the earnest men who had chosen to do so. Particularly when, having reached their pensions, they meddled in local good works and mischief. He knew exactly what this man would be asking; he'd be asking for money to help his Untouchables.

The Man was shaken by a rare moment of anger. What right had any European to come to him and prate of caste? European societies were falling to pieces, riddled by the worm of class warfare, but caste had held Hind together for centuries, two millennia at least, maybe more, and the probability of more to come if fools didn't undermine the foundations.

He sent the Englishman away empty-handed. He didn't approve of subversive doctrines, far less was he prepared to finance them.

The Man spent the rest of the day at his office, attending to the affairs of his interlocking empire. A secretary told him a date had been cancelled and he accepted this with his normal calm. Indeed he had more than half expected it for his caller had been an American banker and such people had their own queer protocol. He was playing hard to get. Then let him. If he had business in India, serious business, he'd be obliged to see Manerji sooner or later.

He used this unusual half hour of leisure to consider his own increasing problems. A European might have thought of bad luck but the term had a special meaning for Manerji. Your luck had been written, was there and immutable, a matter for the advice of astrologers. If things turned out badly they'd got their sums wrong. All you could do was change your astrologers.

In the evening he was driven home. He took his ritual bath and changed his clothes, then asked that his wife should be sent to join him. This was the time of the day they normally talked.

She came to him in a shabby sitting room and they sat facing each other in ancient armchairs. There was a sofa but that was strictly for visitors. It would have been unseemly to sit together, touching. He noticed that she had changed from her finery.

'I've been thinking about what you said this morning.'

She didn't answer this but nodded.

'I intend to be very careful in the future.'

She nodded again but she didn't believe him. She thought him a very fine man, she respected him. He had given her children, a home and security. These she had wanted and for these she was grateful, but she could read him like a childhood book and she knew when he was lying perfectly. Manerji wasn't going to be careful, Manerji had some foolishness brewing in a world where he could misjudge things badly.

She wondered why he bothered with drugs—they were

more than rich enough already. She was an Indian and shrewd and practical; she saw through Manerji like glass. This man of hers, her lawful husband, had very great virtues and from these she had profited. But in business he could do almost anything but behave with a sensible moderation.

For once she had got it slightly wrong; Manerji wasn't thinking of drugs. For the moment that side had turned sour and unprofitable—three killings were an adequate warning. There was another side and that more dangerous. His wife had been right: the Presence was after him. If that Bill went through he'd be finished finally, stripped of his empire by nationalization, a man with a small pension if lucky.

For that he had a plan, a good one. Heroin could go into cold storage. Later, perhaps when the pressure came off. . . .

Meanwhile he had to defeat the Presence and he knew of only one way to do that. Somebody would have to displace it and Manerji thought he knew whom to back. That Kashmiri, under his cloak of loyalty, had his eyes on the throne and meant to have it. He'd taken the first secret steps already, but for the rest he would need a great deal of money. Manerji had money, so there it was.

2

Charles Russell had come with extreme reluctance. He hadn't spent very much time in India but his period there had been long enough. There'd been men he had liked and even half trusted, and Venkata had been emphatically one of them; but on the whole he hadn't been made for India. His own fault of course—he'd admit that freely. His family had never served there, he hadn't any roots to draw down to. He had looked at the country with cool detachment, not the love of a man who came by tradition; and what he had seen had not enchanted him.

And as he flew through the boring night to Delhi he saw that if there was any change that change was on the surface only. The captain came through to chat to the passengers, but only to those with first class tickets. He talked with an inimitable mixture of patronage and commercial subservience. The stewardesses glided smoothly, smiling their gilded asexual smiles and bringing you food and drink at fixed times, the ritual accepted as real.

As he climbed stiffly from the aircraft next morning he noticed a row of taps and men washing. He counted eight taps in a row, eight men under them. Forty yards distant were two more taps and a different sort of man was using them. Illegal no doubt, even unconstitutional. But nobody paid the slightest attention. Charles Russell had not expected they would do. This was the country's strength. It never changed.

He took a taxi to his hotel and slept.

At five he went to Venkata's office, not wholly surprised at what he saw. Security and Intelligence were matters which everyone knew were necessary, but the ordinary man didn't wish to think of them so their practitioners were housed unobtrusively. In America it was quite the opposite, an enormous, flamboyant and hideous building, even notices on the road to guide you there. He himself had worked in London in a discreet old Georgian house in a cul-de-sac. Russell nodded in recognition and went in.

He was taken at once to Venkata's room. They shook hands and sat down, each refreshing his memory. Venkata, Russell thought, hadn't changed much. Madrassis stayed much the same after forty, putting on a little weight which didn't affect their lightning-fast brains. Venkata thought of Colonel Charles Russell that nothing had changed in the man that mattered. His hair had gone grey but he still had all of it, and for a man in late middle age he moved springily. Venkata said:

'An honour to see you, sir.'

'After I've spoken you may not think so.' He had decided how to handle Venkata. Any attempt at over-subtlety and he'd be easily outgunned and defeated. He was going to lay them down and he did so. Venkata said at the end:

'You do not surprise me.'

'That a drug ring is controlled from India?'

'I *know* that a drug ring is run from India. The name of the man who runs it is Manerji, the one they often call the Man. Personally I detest the whole business.'

'Then why don't you clean it up?'

'I do not dare.'

'Politics?' Russell asked sympathetically. He knew all about the crippling connection between politics and what ought to be done.

'The last thing this country could ever afford would be an international scandal in drugs. You know how the Presence values our image—high-thinking, low-living, as white as snow.' Venkata spoke without hint of cynicism, stating a truth which was known to both. 'Perhaps,' he added, his voice unchanged, 'perhaps it's a trifle smug for some.'

Charles Russell laughed; he liked this Madrassi, the man was a realist. 'Does Manerji ever visit England?'

'Quite often when he has business there. The next time he does so I'll let you know.'

'There's politics in England too.'

'I wasn't thinking of an English court. I have half an idea but I've not worked it out.' He waved at his desk which was littered with papers. 'I'm under a bit of pressure just now.'

'I understand,' Charles Russell said, and indeed he understood very well. The Drug Squad was undermanned —King had said so—and Security was not much better. The money went on what caught the votes.

Venkata pointed at his desk again. 'Can you wait a few days till I've got that clear?'

'I can wait as long as you wish.'

'That's kind. Will you leave me your address?'

'Of course.' Russell named a hotel and Venkata noted it;

he said in at tone of polite surprise:

'That isn't the best hotel in Delhi.'

'I seldom stay at the best hotels. Stay at the best hotels and you're miserable. Jerusalem, Rio — they're indistinguishable. Besides, I don't like ice in my water.'

'I'll ring you, then — I promise that.'

As they moved to the door the Madrassi said softly:

'Does Manerji know you're here?'

'Why should he?'

'He's a man with very good sources.'

Charles Russell shrugged.

When Russell had left him Venkata telephoned. He greatly admired this English Colonel, wishing him well and above all safety. But money like Manerji's could buy almost anything. Venkata gave clear precise orders and he gave them in his own soft language. Like any other Indian he much preferred to use his own people.

He lit a cheroot and pulled on it thoughtfully. He'd been wanting a smoke for some time but hadn't liked to. He smoked villainous black Burmese cheroots and he knew that Charles Russell was more particular. He didn't keep cigarettes, he detested them. So he'd simply gone without his cheroot.

He inhaled the potent smoke but didn't cough. Money, he thought again, great wealth. It was a line which hadn't so far struck him but now he considered it more than promising. He took paper and started to write it down, a habit he'd learnt from his British mentors.

1. *That Kashmiri is making his run for power and he's going to need the finance to do it. A great deal of finance to build a power base, to buy the marginal but vital support which I doubt if he has as he stands today.*

2. *He isn't a rich man himself in spite of all his upper class airs, so somebody will have to back him. And that somebody must have a motive.*

3. *Manerji? Manerji has a powerful motive. He's frightened of more nationalization and he knows that the*

Presence hates his guts. If that Kashmiri reaches power on Manerji's money the pressure would come off him at once.

He considered this over his stinking butt. It was sodden and he threw it away.

4. *In any case my first duty is clear. It is to stop the Kashmiri by any means possible.*

He looked gloomily at the papers before him. He had had the same problem before and knew no answer. It was the easiest country in all the world in which to obtain your information, the hardest in which to assess its value. Anyone would delate on anyone, for race or caste hatred, for land, or money. The false rumour was part of the dusty air, and the head of the political Bureau must evaluate what came before him by training and a long experience, above all things by the delicate instincts of a man who trusted no other completely.

He looked at the mass of papers on his desk, considered the whispers which reached him covertly. All of them came to one thing, if established. He had wondered about him before—that Kashmiri. He'd been put on the committee of four, probably to keep him occupied, but he was too clever by far and much too ambitious to stay content for long with a second class job such as trying to break a man like Manerji. So now he was making his run for power, to displace the Presence and take over the country.

Venkata didn't wish this to happen. The Presence was invariably arrogant, sometimes unjust and always ruthless, but it had what no other in India held, the flair to keep the frail house of cards standing. Remove it and there could well be chaos, and only his own, the Dravidian south, had a chance that it might go it alone. Venkata didn't want that for he was proud of his country. Somebody had told him once that no country was ever really free unless it had fought for its independence. Well, they'd fought all right, though not with arms, and somehow they'd held together since. Someday the Presence would have to go, there'd have to be some sort of successor, but at this moment a coup would be utter disaster.

Especially one by that damned Kashmiri. Venkata had never liked him, his patrician airs and social graces, his only half concealed contempt for this dark little man who'd come up from the south. Venkata was an Indian, politics were in his blood. He understood the Kashmiri perfectly.

Venkata looked at another report. The Kashmiri was going up to an ashram, a fashionable la-di-dah one. Manerji sometimes went there too, and if their next visits coincided Venkata would know what to do. Nevertheless there were practical difficulties. He couldn't go there himself since he wasn't smart enough, and in any case his unexplained presence would raise eyebrows and put men on their guard. He had a competent and qualified agent, but he too would look strange and out of place in what amounted to a country club for the richer of the New Delhi establishment.

He sighed at a sudden sardonic thought. Now Colonel Russell would have been ideal, the distinguished European visitor interested in the resident guru.

Of course he couldn't suggest it, though. He couldn't ask Colonel Russell to plant a bug.

Manerji was now in his splendid office, the one in the brash new town which he hated. He was wearing European clothes, which he hated too but had learnt to tolerate, except for the shoes which he still found a misery. He wore these clothes because he must. He had connections all over the world and they came to him, men from the States, West Germany, England. It wouldn't do to receive these visitors dressed in a dhoti and comfortable sandals, a caricature of a village bunniah. He had once seen a man in New York in a kilt. At first he had smiled but had then felt embarrassed, not for himself but for the professional Scot. When in Rome you did as the Romans did, and this importantly furnished room was Rome. In his house he would wear the clothes he found comfortable but in office hours he'd make wise concessions. So he sat in his expensive suit and he looked at the desk diary before him. It was much too crowded. That secretary was getting slack. He was a nephew, naturally, but not indispensable. The Man decided that he must speak to him sharply.

And Manerji had a mounting worry. The Presence was putting increasing pressure on, it was whittling his empire down to nothing; it had carved away great slices already and the rest would be only a question of time.

That is if the Presence were still alive.

Manerji sent for sweet tea and drank it. The Kashmiri was going up to an ashram so Manerji would go there too. It would be an excellent place for secret business.

Meanwhile that American banker hadn't called. Manerji had been sure he would, that he'd been playing hard to get and no more. But no, he had sent a polite little note. The matter they'd meant to discuss could be interesting, but the banker must consult his colleagues. If they found themselves in substantial agreement the banker would let Mr Manerji know.

Manerji would have confessed to some pique. He wasn't some importunate salesman to be dismissed with a promise to think it over, and if playing hard to get was the game, he considered that this American banker was overplaying it uncharacteristically. But perhaps he had really left Delhi.

Check it.

Manerji knew where the American stayed, a modest hotel which was called the Weybridge. It had been English-owned and was still English-run, an egg-and-bacony sort of place but comfortable. Manerji had always been mildly surprised that Wallace Noorlander, President of the Noorlander Bank, should choose the Weybridge for his occasional visits, but he did so and any check must start there.

He sent the senior of his several secretaries, a conscientious, babu-ish man who was also very frightened of

Manerji. Manerji could often be exigent, and if the babu returned with the simple answer 'Not there' Manerji was as likely as not to frown and ask him how he'd made sure.

The babu gave the receptionist two hundred rupees for a list of everyone presently staying. He'd have to fiddle it from the office float since the Man was outrageously mean about trifles.

When Manerji saw the list he froze. Mr. Wallace Noorlander wasn't on it but a man called Colonel Charles Russell was.

Manerji called for his car and was driven home. He thought better at home and thought was imperative.

They were really going after him now. First those Sikhs who hadn't mattered much, and then Sen who had mattered a great deal more. Fenwick was powerful, not a man to be trifled with, and with Russell the Man had already tangled, not over drugs but indirectly. And Russell had outguessed and outsmarted him. The Man had a healthy respect for Russell.

Who would hardly have come to Delhi on holiday, certainly not in the height of the summer.

And whatever might be his plans for mischief he had chosen the most embarrassing moment. If Manerji and that fancy Kashmiri couldn't come to terms to their mutual advantage Manerji stood to lose his shirt to an implacable Presence who hated him bitterly—Manerji and all that he stood for, free enterprise, great wealth, the lot. And all to what he considered a theory, a theory for idealistic halfwits.

. . . Russell. He wasn't easily frightened. That had been tried and it hadn't worked. But anything more drastic? Dangerous. The Man had turned that down once before. If Russell died by some act of violence there'd be more than local curiosity. Quiet men with an air of quiet authority would gather from unexpected places, there'd be very much worse than an Indian hush-up, there'd be a solid professional sifting of evidence. And the scent could only lead one way.

On the other hand if the Presence weren't there, if the Kashmiri sat in its august place, Manerji's creature, indebted to Manerji . . . .

He thought it over, tense and concentrated. It was a choice of risks but a choice had been forced on him. Finally he made up his mind. Like Venkata he gave clear crisp orders.

Charles Russell thought his day well spent. There was nothing concrete yet and he hadn't expected it, but he hadn't been cold-shouldered rudely, his address had been asked for and carefully noted. And there was something else though not precise words for it. But Charles Russell's antennae were highly developed and they'd told him something he didn't doubt. Quite apart from the pile of work on his desk Venkata had some private crisis, though it was nothing whatever to do with drugs.

Very well, so Charles Russell would have to wait patiently.

He dined off what the Weybridge called curry, done English fashion and therefore indifferent, and by half past eleven was fast asleep.

He didn't know how long he'd been sleeping when something woke him, not noise but its absence. The Weybridge was an old-fashioned hotel which hadn't got round to air conditioning. It had ceiling fans which, in Russell's opinion, were as good and certainly far more airy, and the one in Russell's room had a fault. It clicked rhythmically, not enough to stop sleep, but sufficient to impose its own pattern. Russell woke when the pattern stopped. As had the fan.

Charles Russell swore. Another current cut.

He lay with his hands behind his head. The open window was in front of him and there was light in the hotel's compound outside. Not a great deal of light but enough to define. To define a man's head as it cleared the window sill.

The head was wearing a hood.

Russell stiffened. He wasn't armed for he seldom was. He saw an arm coming up below the head.

He rolled fast to his left, out of bed, to the floor. A bullet thumped into the bedhead above him. Simultaneously there was another shot. This one was outside the room. The head at the window had disappeared.

He crawled towards the window cautiously, then even more cautiously raised his head. There was more light in the compound now, lamps and men. Two were loading a third on a canvas stretcher, another standing guard above them. Russell could see his rifle clearly. It was modern with a modern night sight. The little party of four, three living, one dead, began to move away at a trot. They moved towards a decaying hedge, disappearing through a convenient gap. Charles Russell's hearing was still acute and he heard what he thought were van doors opening, the noise of the stretcher sliding in. Then the doors as they shut and the engine starting. For a moment they revved it, then noise faded away.

. . . That was very slick work, very neat indeed. He'd told Fenwick he had a friend in India and this friend's friends were clearly extremely competent.

There was nothing more he could do with real purpose but he shut the open window thoughtfully. The fan had not come on again and it was going to be very hot without it. Russell went peacefully back to his bed but it was longer than usual before he slept again.

He woke rather early and sat waiting for tea, but just as the waiter was bringing it in the telephone by his bedside rang noisily.

'Colonel Russell?' The voice was Indian and clearly anxious. Russell recognized it as Venkata's but it wasn't Venkata's ordinary voice.

'Good morning Mr. Venkata.'

'So you *are* all right, they told me you were. I needn't tell you I was relieved to hear it.'

'I imagine I owe you my life. I'm grateful. Any small service. . . .'

'May I come over?'

'At any time you wish.'

'I'll come now.'

Venkata arrived very promptly. Things had begun to go his way. He'd known the Kashmiri often visited that trendy ashram and he'd suspected and indeed had hoped that Manerji might be going there too. Now he knew that they'd be there together. The Bureau might be housed unobtrusively but it wasn't kept so short of funds that it couldn't check on Manerji's movements. So Manerji and that haughty Kashmiri were going to be at the ashram together. Those two visits might be only coincidence but Venkata didn't think they were. The Man was staying for only a single night but the single night would be plenty to fix things.

In the car he began to relax a little, for the events of the night before had dealt him a card. He'd been puzzling how to bug that ashram and now he had his answer pat. Charles Russell would do it, or rather his servant would. Charles Russell would be entirely acceptable and by established custom he'd take a servant. That servant would be Venkata's man, the best of his several carefully trained agents. Charles Russell wouldn't kick at that; Charles Russell had talked of any small service.

A bargain, Venkata thought, a deal. The deal was in his veins and viscera and he'd reached where he was by making good ones.

They discussed the night's incident coolly and briefly, almost with the weariness of men who had seen it all before. Then Venkata said:

'I'm asking a favour.'

As he'd expected, Russell answered at once. 'I owe you one.'

'Then here it is.' He explained his plan for the ashram quickly.

Charles Russell nodded. 'So I'm the front man.'

'He's a very good agent indeed—my best. He's an ex-havildar from the cream of our regiments which takes men from only forty-two families. His name is Shinday—I think you'll like him. He wouldn't get by at that ashram alone but with you as his cover he'll pass as a servant. He's a first class shot as you've probably guessed and on top of that he has adequate English.' Venkata allowed a brief smile. 'By the way, he's quite good at being a servant. You'll find that your clothes are kept impeccably.'

'Quite a man. And the bug?'

'That will be Shinday's business, not yours. They're easy enough to plant, as you know—men have to eat and go to the loo—but as you'll also know it's not always so easy to get them out fast when most you need to. Men will natter at night without thought, but sometimes in the morning they start to wonder. They start poking about to try to find things and there won't be time for searchproof concealment.'

Russell nodded again. This was reassuring. It was professional talk between two professionals.

'So there'll have to be some slight distraction. Round about midnight, I rather fancy.'

'What sort of distraction?'

'One to amuse you. At least I hope so.'

Venkata went off to his office happily. This was India, the land of the backscratch, and he'd just achieved a rather neat one. It was also a country you couldn't hurry. The pace of the bullock cart was three miles an hour but the Bureau could move faster than that.

He began to put his plan in motion.

3

He had fixed it in twenty-four hours, it was ticking. Shinday was climbing from Russell's car, leaving it well below the ashram since cars were still not allowed to defile it. He picked up his master's casual suitcase and both of them began to walk.

Venkata had chosen well, for Shinday was broad-shouldered and wiry, the typical Mahratta uplander. He was smiling in anticipation, for the lush pastures of this degenerate ashram held fat cattle for a virile man. . . . All those extraordinary European women with their saris and sandals and marks of marriage which they were very seldom entitled to wear. . . . He had heard all about it from friends and believed it. They were tiresomely earnest but some also pretty, and most of the men who came here were elderly. Shinday stroked his moustache reflectively. He knew he was a good-looking man and the pickings would be a generous bonus to an assignment which he'd accepted eagerly. Manerji was another Marwadi whom Mahrattas had excellent reason to hate, and the Kashmiri was like all Kashmiris, a man who could contrive an intrigue from two birds on a lawn and a piece of bread.

It was a mile up the dusty path and steep but he didn't relax his light infantry pace. Presently Russell said: 'Not so fast. Drop it to a hundred and twenty.'

The ex-havildar dropped it to a hundred and ten. He was proud of his light infantry marching but he could see that Charles Russell was no longer a boy.

They rounded a bend and there it was. Russell stopped and stared in unblinking astonishment. In his earlier days in this very strange country 'ashram' had been a word of precision; it had stood for a place of religious reflection, almost a place of pious pilgrimage if the man at its head were sufficiently famous, a place of string beds and the minimum diet.

But this one didn't look like that. Russell knew that in the background somewhere was a man who called himself the guru, but he was known to be a total fraud. And accepted as a fraud—that was the point. The ashram was still an ashram in name since that was an accepted tradition, but the huts had gone and the charpoy beds, the air of an abrasive austerity. Instead there were bungalows, neat and new, with verandahs and long chairs and tables. There was a bathhouse and showers and proper lavatories (some even had European seats, he had heard) and in the background, incredibly, well-kept tennis courts. Russell could catch the smell of cooking and it certainly wasn't chapattis or rice. The garden was green and the lawn well watered.

A woman came mincing out to meet him. 'Colonel Russell?' she asked.

'Mr Russell here.'

'I'm glad you don't use your military rank.'

Russell thought the remark both priggish and stupid and he'd noticed the American accent. East coast, he rather thought. He was right. She had a tiny and very elegant waist which emphasized her existing endowments like a figure in some ageless temple. She wore a sari and sandals, her brown hair in a bun, but no mark on her forehead to tell a lie. He gave her a good mark for that. She was every sort of misguided fool but at least she wasn't a vulgar cheat.

'May I take you to your room?' she said.

He followed her across the compound to a bungalow with a long verandah. She walked like an Italian woman, erect but swaying her nates freely. They went up the verandah steps and she unlocked the door of a bedroom which gave on it. She stood aside and said: 'After you.'

'By no means. You go first.' He was firm.

She smiled and went first, not displeased at his manner. This wasn't the visitors' normal form, and it was nice to be treated for once like a lady.

The room was simply but comfortably furnished, a mile from the ashram's original ethos. There was a European bed with a mattress, and the sheets on it were clean and inviting. Shinday had followed and unpacked quickly. Then he slipped away and Russell knew where. He hadn't had a smoke all day and in the servants' godowns he'd surely find one. It seemed to do him no harm whatever, but then it was a long way from heroin.

The woman had meanwhile stood by quietly, hands folded in her lap, eyes down. Now she said:

'Shall I turn on the punkah?'

Russell hadn't noticed the ceiling fan, and more than anything else he had seen that day it struck him as the great betrayal.

'No thank you, it's quite cool up here. But perhaps you could open the windows.'

'Gladly.'

When she came back he asked her quietly: 'May I know your name?'

'I'm called Sanogita.'

'Your real one, I meant.'

'I'm Sanogita here.'

'But I think I shall call you Mary just the same.'

'And how did you know?'

'I didn't—I guessed.' He could see that she wasn't at all offended.

She was suddenly very American, businesslike.

'The Master will see you at midnight exactly.'

Midnight, he thought—that would do very well. For at midnight there would be a distraction and he didn't want to see the Master. He had prepared some rather foolish questions and the answers would no doubt be even more foolish. The distraction, whatever it be, would be welcome but for the moment he must keep up appearances. He said to the woman:

'Will you take me to him?'

'I will if you wish it.'

'I'll need an hour to prepare.' He knew the form.

'That's perfectly normal. And you're expected to fast before you see him.'

'I know that too.' He had done his homework. Russell, who disapproved of fasting, had some sandwiches which he'd hidden cunningly.

'Is there anything else I can do?'

'No thank you.'

'But I think I'll just tidy the bed.'

She did so. He was standing on one side, she the other. As she bent over, her sari swung open. She wasn't wearing the bodice which went with a sari but a mischievous, very American bra. Her breasts weren't big but were wholly delicious. She straightened as though she'd done nothing deliberate.

'And afterwards we'll discuss it comfortably.'

'With pleasure,' he said. He felt safe in saying so. There wasn't going to be an afterwards. He wondered if ex-havildar Shinday, somewhere in the servants' quarters, was receiving the same considerate room service. Almost certainly yes, Charles Russell decided. He was a very handsome man indeed.

Shinday came in with a well-pressed suit and Russell said: 'Good evening, Colour.' He knew this flattered Shinday greatly.

Shinday said: 'Sir,' and watched his front.

'Any news on the local form?'

'A little. I've already found out where their rooms are.'

'Good. But which room are they going to use to talk?'

'They must use the Kashmiri's.' Shinday sounded a little surprised. 'The Kashmiri wouldn't demean himself by going to a bunniah's bedroom.'

'Even today?'

'You don't know Kashmiris.'

'Bug planted yet?'

'I shall wait till they're eating.'

'Relay on station?'

'The van's up in the wood.'

'You're a very well trained soldier.'

'Sir.'

'So all we have to wait for now is the little distraction Mr.

Venkata promised.'

'At a quarter to twelve.'

'Thank God for that.'

'Sir?' It was a question now.

'I've a appointment with that fraud at midnight and afterwards one which I fancy still less.'

The ex-havildar made a curious gesture. Charles Russell hadn't seen it before but he reckoned he could read it; he said:

'Unfortunately she doesn't attract me.'

'I'm sorry, sir. I'm very sorry.'

He was evidently better suited himself.

Russell had eaten his ample sandwiches, then dozed in a long cane chair outside. He had a tiny alarm in his wrist watch and set it; he set it for quarter to midnight. And at eleven forty-five precisely pandemonium broke loose uncontrollably. A bungalow was burning fiercely and Russell, who knew something of fires, watched it with a detached curiosity. Normally fires took hold fairly slowly, even in wooden buildings like this one, but this bungalow had gone up like a torch, simultaneously at both ends and the middle.

. . . That Shinday has been excellently taught.

The flames threw a lurid glare and Russell stared. After the cool, almost clinical incident in the compound of the Weybridge hotel there was only one word for this. It was atavism. Men and women were running in fruitless panic, there was a babel of Hindi in varied accents. No Urdu. Muslims didn't patronize ashrams. One man had an extinguisher, but it hadn't been serviced and didn't work. A second had his dhoti smouldering and was screaming as another threw water. He went on screaming: the other had missed. Finally he fell down and rolled. The screaming stopped—the burn hadn't been serious. Beyond a flower-bed two figures were inexplicably fighting. They reversed their positions and Russell frowned. They weren't, as he'd supposed, two men, but a man and a woman struggling fiercely. There wasn't any sign of Shinday, which meant that he'd probably done what he wished to before the fire had spread and made it too dangerous. He'd have known where to look since he'd made the plant, and he was a man who could move very quickly indeed.

By now the bungalow had almost burnt out. The singed-dhoti man was still gesticulating, a knot of other men around him. Nobody had been trapped inside and nobody seemed to be seriously hurt. When the bungalow was a smouldering wreck two men appeared with an ancient fire hose. One turned on the nozzle. No water came.

Russell went inside to laugh. He could see now why Venkata hadn't told him. Venkata had a Madrassi's humour and he hadn't wanted to spoil the fun.

4

When he'd checked that the tapes had recorded properly and that the van had been removed to safety, Shinday drove back to Delhi fast. He went at once to Venkata's office.

'Have a good time?' the latter asked.

'Very pleasant, thank you. Very pleasant indeed.' His manner with Venkata was less formally military than it had been with Russell, but he was still respectful. Venkata paid his salary and Shinday had an uncontemporary respect for the man who found the money which fed him.

Venkata had expected it. Shinday was really extremely handsome. 'What have you brought me?'

'These tapes for one thing.' He put them down. 'The story's all there in a good deal of detail, but I can put it in a couple of sentences.' He did so with a quiet precision. 'Manerji will stake the Kashmiri in an attempt to overthrow the Presence. That I rather think you suspected but I don't think you suspected the method. It's going to be by assassination.

If Shinday had hoped to create a sensation he wasn't in any way disappointed. Venkata strode round the shabby room. It was far too hot for uncalled for exercise, and he was a man who sweated extremely easily. The Kashmiri had noticed it once and looked away . . . this coarse little, dark little, man with the glistening face, the cotton handkerchief with which he had wiped it. The Kashmiri had dabbed at his own with silk.

A political assassination. There'd been another not so long ago and it had almost torn the country to pieces. A second at this particular moment would inevitably do just that. Venkata asked at last:

'You're sure?'

'It's all in those tapes. You can run them at leisure.'

Venkata sat down rather heavily. For the first time in his life he felt his age. He hadn't seen it going like this, it threw his timetable from a skyscraper's penthouse. The Kashmiri, he'd thought, would need weeks, maybe months—time to manoeuvre, to fix, and suborn, to build up an effective power base from which to make an orthodox challenge. But a killing could take place at any time.

It could happen as they sat there discussing it.

Shinday knew this too and was asking: 'What do we do now? Pull him in?'

Venkata shook his head regretfully. There were plenty of Emergency Powers, more men in jail without trial than was published, but Venkata was hamstrung again, inhibited as he had been with Manerji by the fear of a resounding scandal. The Kashmiri might need to build up his power base before he could make a run for power, but he was a figure in his own right already, too big to pick up and tuck away quietly. And those tapes alone wouldn't swing a Court, they'd had more than one spurious tape already.

'Any line on the killer?'

'Nothing which you could call a line. I think the Kashmiri must have someone in mind but long before he came round to names the Man shut him up with a bang you could hear.'

'Typical,' Venkata said contemptuously. Planning a killing was quite in order but knowing the details was something else. There were plenty of people like that. He despised them. 'Any ideas yourself?'

'Only vague ones. It might be some wretched Pakistani.'

'That would probably mean war again.'

'Oh, I didn't mean a proper Pakky, I meant one of those wretched East Bengalis.' Shinday, a Mahratta, thought little of them. 'I suppose I should call them Bengladeshis, but whatever word you use to describe them there are plenty who are very bitter. When we chopped them off from Pakistan they thought we were going to take them over. Very wisely we didn't, we left them to stew. No lush pickings from Mother India — none. There were men who believed they'd be well paid puppets but instead of that they're back in their jute fields.'

'You think that some East Bengali *thug*' — he pronounced it the Indian way and meant it — 'you really believe some Bengali cut-throat could be bribed to have a go at the Presence?'

'It was only a suggestion, sir.'

'Then make me another and make it a better one.'

'Then what about those other people whom the Blacks decided to throw out of Africa? The English got lumbered with most of those but one or two of them foolishly chanced it here. They had families but they brought no money so the families weren't pleased to see them. Many are walking around near starving.' Shinday shook his head in sorrow. 'Sometimes I think that we're not nice people.'

'But most of that lot were Guzeratis. You're a Mahratta, you should talk more sense. Till the British came you used to plunder them regularly. A Guzerati will hardly kill a fly, not even for money and God knows they love it. In any case it doesn't matter since we haven't a name of any kind, nobody we could pull in and break.'

Shinday said slowly: 'Which leaves an alternative.'

'I was thinking that too.'

'Would you authorize irreversible action?'

'Could you do it yourself?'

'Oh yes, very easily.' Shinday added with apparent irrelevance: 'It's lucky that Kashmiri rides a bicycle.'

'Bicycle?'

'It's all part of his image. His backing is on the Right, you know, the old men who never learn and never forget, the old has-beens in homespun clothes and funny hats. They think motor-cars are a wild extravagance and anyway they're not really Indian. The Kashmiri plays up to that lot madly. When he needs a car he hires a taxi but he bicycles to his office daily.'

'Which could be dangerous in Delhi's traffic.'

'I'm sure it's very risky indeed.' Shinday began to get up.

'Sit down.' It was an order given smilingly for Venkata approved of Shinday. If this was the New India, then perhaps there was a shadow of hope for her. 'Now listen to me. No premature action.' He lit another of his formidable cheroots. 'So I'll listen to your tapes with great care.'

'And what do I do till you give me orders?'

'Use your evident talent for picking up news. Prepare your ground quietly for possible action. Obviously you must keep your mouth shut since if anything went wrong we'd be compromised. And don't let anyone beat you to it.'

Six hours later he rang back to Shinday. 'You have clearance,' he said.

'I'm delighted to hear it.'

Shinday had made his preparations, which he hadn't found hard since they hadn't been complicated. Basically they had been to discover the time when the Kashmiri left his home for his office, and that had been very easy indeed. It had been almost as easy to steal a car, for Shinday knew where they stood for the taking, outside a Scandinavian embassy.

They weren't guarded except by an elderly watchman, since the philosophy of this smug little embassy would never have allowed an armed guard in a country which it wooed ostentatiously. Moreover, the cars were mostly Volvos and Shinday had once owned a Volvo himself. He still had a key though it might not fit, but Venkata hadn't needed to tell him where to go for the keys of all recent Volvos.

He dealt with the elderly watchman gently, frightening him much more than he hurt him, then he put on gloves and chose a car. The third key he tried was a fit.

He drove away.

The Kashmiri had woken in an excellent temper for he'd had news of a man who might serve his purpose. He naturally couldn't recruit him directly, but there had reached him through his fog of cover, his agents, half agents and hangers-on, the name of a man who might very well do. He was a European who needed money badly, the son of a man whose prosperous business had kicked at increasing demands for protection and had therefore finally gone to the wall. He wanted to get out of India and he wanted the money to start elsewhere. His price was apparently far too high, but the Kashmiri knew the answer to that. You promised what was asked and paid part of it. Only a very stupid man would suppose such a promise would be kept to the letter and a stupid and desperate man would do desperate things.

So the Kashmiri was in a very good temper. Only two trifles nagged his good humour: one was his ridiculous clothes, the other this undignified bicycle. He had eaten his breakfast wrapped in a dressing gown, a handsome affair of expensive silk, but afterwards he had changed into homespun. He must wear it for a little longer since the men of the Right gave him credit for doing so, but he wouldn't need these men for ever, and when he was firmly seated in power he would wear what he fancied, which was a good English suit. Moreover, the suit would be made in London, not by some journeyman tailor locally.

And the bicycle was even more irritating. He looked a charley on a bicycle, like some babu pedalling down to his office. He'd have to suffer it, though, for a little longer, till he'd reached where he'd always meant to go. Then the bicycle and this uncomfortable uniform could be thrown onto a bonfire together.

He called his servant who held the bicycle upright. The Kashmiri wasn't good at bicycles. He didn't mount them as most people did, by putting one foot on a pedal and swinging over. There was a step on the back axle instead and the Kashmiri clambered up on it shakily. The servant held the bicycle firmly, then, when his master was settled, ran alongside. Presently, with a little momentum, the Kashmiri said to his servant: 'Let go.'

The servant did so and stood aside. The performance had never ceased to amaze him, but he was much too good a servant to say so.

The Kashmiri wobbled down a short drive, then turned left in a residential road. It was early and there was little traffic, but near the centre it would increase alarmingly. This was the part the Kashmiri hated, but on this day which had started with smiling stars he didn't get anywhere near the centre.

Shinday had been cruising quietly on the streets which enclosed his target's bungalow. When he saw him first he was well in front and hitting from the back was uncertain. He passed the Kashmiri without a glance, slipping into a lane and turning. He was utterly without emotion; he was doing a job and it didn't trouble him. He didn't admire the Presence blindly but undeniably it had done much for his country, and its handling of those East Bengalis had been a triumph of coolly brilliant diplomacy backed up by overwhelming force at a moment which had been perfectly chosen. Moreover he disliked the Kashmiri; he disliked any man who would kill by proxy. He was a soldier by race and a soldier by training. Hiring assassins was plainly dishonourable and men of dishonour could ask no mercy. He drove back into the main road deliberately.

. . . Eighty yards to the plodding bicycle. Plenty.

The Kashmiri, head down, didn't see the Volvo till it was less than forty yards away from him. Then he saw the C. D. plates and swore. These wretched diplomats, nobodies really, could drive in cars and very few questioned it, but he who would shortly rule this country was constrained to use this preposterous bicycle lest foolish old men thought him self-indulgent. It was puritanism gone mad, sheer masochism, and he knew whose ghost he must blame for that. For the moment, though, he didn't dare to. Later, when he was firmly in power, he'd start telling the truth and the New Men would listen.

At what point his anger changed to terror was something which no man would ever know. The Volvo was going fast, accelerating, raising a cloud of dust he must plod through. He swore again but stopped swearing suddenly. The Volvo had swung at him, suddenly, wickedly. For an instant he didn't believe what he saw, then a single despairing cry came out of him. The driver of the Volvo straightened.

On the pavement behind what was left of a man were two clerks with umbrellas, walking demurely. They saw an accident and began to run. It was instinctive, a conditioned reflex. There'd be inquiries, depositions, the police. They didn't desire the least involvement. Every man had to die at some time.

On the other side of the road was a bullock cart. Shinday had passed it making his run but he hadn't in any way feared its presence. For he had known what the driver would do, and he did it. He neither stopped nor turned his head. The bullock cart went on at three miles an hour.

The Kashmiri lay in the road unconscious and his lifeblood ran away in the gutter.

5

When Shinday had slipped away from the ashram Russell had waited for forty-eight hours. Venkata would need time to consider and Russell was very short of exercise. He took it walking the cool, wooded hills, then returned to the heat and dust of Delhi.

The summons, when it came, was welcome. Venkata received him formally but Russell could see he was much more relaxed. He also noticed that his desk was clear. A wall between them had quietly fallen: Venkata was going to play ball. He said when Russell was comfortably settled:

'There was a plot in this country to murder the Presence. A Kashmiri intended to take over power and the man who was going to finance the Kashmiri is also the man in whom you're interested.'

'Political assassination? All good officers have a duty to block it.'

'I have done so in the only way possible.' He said it coolly, he was quite unashamed. He and Charles Russell shared the same background. 'Have you seen the newspapers?'

Russell considered before he answered. Venkata was setting a very hot pace. He was an Indian and could surely be devious but he'd put down a card and had probably more. It was an invitation to play the hand out straight and Russell was very glad to accept it.

'There was a headline that a well-known Kashmiri, a politician in the highest class—'

'Had met with an unfortunate accident. Quite so. That is over and done with. Leave it. Let's return to that man in whom we're both interested.' He accepted one of Charles Russell's cigars. 'These are wasted on me really.'

'Never mind.'

Venkata opened a drawer and gave Russell a file. 'That's a copy file on Manerji. Keep it. Read it and wonder. Read it and hate.'

'You hate him too?'

'Of course I do. I don't hate him because he's rich and powerful, I don't hate him for the Presence's reasons; I loathe him because he traffics in drugs and I was a policeman before they gave me the Bureau. So I'll tell you when he next goes to England.'

'And I told you that in England too there are politics which often conflict with action.'

'I remember you did and I understood perfectly. But I don't want him sent to an English prison, far less do I want to see him killed there. Killing is much to good for Manerji. I want him in an Indian prison, humiliated publicly, broken.'

'But by hypothesis you can't do that. You insisted you couldn't face a drug scandal.'

'Perfectly true—I daren't do that. I'm just asking you to set him up.

'Set him up for what?'

Venkata told him and Russell whistled. He'd once had a reputation for ruthlessness but he wasn't in this Madrassi's class.

Venkata went on reflectively. 'It's curious how values change. Once the big crimes were moral crimes, stealing and rape and beating children. Now those are matters for earnest psychiatrists. The worst crimes are fiscal, crimes made in a book. In Russia, for the offence I've just mentioned, you'd spend the rest of a very short life in a labour camp.'

'You're sure it would work?'

'I'm perfectly sure. I can forgive you if you don't understand for I don't think you understand Mother India, or not as she is run today. There are scandals almost every week, fixes and bribes and commissions—everything. They're internal scandals and somehow we live with them, but if the man in that file were arrested here as the drugmaster he undoubtedly is we wouldn't be able to keep it quiet. It would go round the world and shame us miserably; we might even lose most of the Aid which keeps us afloat.

But there's a sin against the Holy Ghost, or there is as we presently live in this country, and if Manerji were caught committing it there wouldn't be any sort of backlash, specifically no foreign backlash. As for any feeling locally, there wouldn't be any feeling at all. He'd simply be a very rich man who'd been trying to get a bit richer meanly. The Courts would feel obliged to be merciless and public opinion would be wholly behind them. He'd get at least eight years and die in prison.'

Russell thought for three minutes, then said at the end of them:

'You're suggesting I fix the English end of it?'

'You think you could do it?'

'Once very easily. Now I shall have to consult with friends.'

'Then I'll let you know when Manerji leaves and I'll send over by hand what our plan will need. We may not be the CIA but we do have certain modest resources.'

'The greatest of them is your own intelligence.'

Venkata rose and shook hands ritually. 'It has been a great honour. I have ventured to book a seat on an evening flight. The happiest of landings, sir.'

'Sincerest thanks for everything.'

'Nothing.'

Venkata put out Russell's cigar. As he'd said, it had in fact been wasted on him, for it had given him no satisfaction whatever. But the morning had—very great satisfaction. It was early for a drink but he took one.

To Russell, he thought as he drank it. To his friend.

FOUR

FOUR

1

Manerji's wife was wearing her warpaint, best sari, her jewellery, all the fixings. He recognized the signals uneasily: they were in for another up-and-downer.

She came straight to the point with the careless candour of a woman who had money behind her. Her family's money was mixed with Manerji's and she wasn't going to stand for nonsense.

'I advised you to be very careful.'

'And I told you that I would be.'

'Have you?'

'I am being very careful indeed.'

She sat down uninvited — almost unprecedented. 'And what about those drugs you sell?'

If she'd hoped to surprise him she didn't succeed for he'd long believed she knew or suspected. . . . The interminable chatter of women of all ages, the dangerous chatter of those past childbearing!

'I have decided to let that matter be.'

Quite exceptionally he was telling the truth. There'd been no hint in the papers and none from his sources that the Sikhs had been carrying drugs when they died, so presumably whoever had killed them had done so for the motive of robbery, but Sen's death would call for more delicate handling, not by himself but by the English authorities. Two Irishmen had been pulled in and questioned and they'd told a very curious story. They'd said that Sen had double-crossed them over payment for frightening William Fenwick. All that had happened later was an accident.

Hm. But why had Sen paid them to frighten Fenwick? Manerji knew the answer to that but the two men who'd been arrested did not. They had told a very different story; they'd confessed they belonged to an Organization, one which hated Fenwick bitterly. . . . Convincing and very probably true, but in that case why had V. S. Sen, Attaché to a High Commission, been meddling in domestic politics by financing these men to act against Fenwick? He had behaved as no diplomatist should, playing with internal affairs, but Sen was most conveniently dead and his foolishness would be discreetly muffled. Drugs wouldn't be mentioned—there wasn't a reason to. The authorities probably knew the truth but were as scared of it as were those in India. So there was going to be a top level smother. The Man was wise in the ways of diplomacy and he hadn't a moment's doubt of that.

But Sir William Fenwick wasn't a diplomat. William Fenwick was still an active danger. So he repeated to his wife:

'I have left it.'

She sat with her jewelled hands folded submissively but submissiveness was not in her heart or intention. She was watching her husband as she'd watched him for years. She was obliged to watch since they seldom spoke freely, and by now she could read the least change in expression, tiny movements of the eyes and lips which nobody but herself would have noticed. She decided that he was telling the truth, his own sort of truth which was never the whole of it. She didn't blame him for this since she did it herself.

'I think you have made a wise decision.'

'Did you come here to tell me that?' He was irritated.

'No, I did not—there is something more serious.' She knew instinctively there was something more serious. This man had been plotting a very great foolishness. She knew his plotting face from experience.

'You'd better tell me,' he said a little wearily.

'The Presence would like to destroy you. I told you before.'

'I remember you did and it wasn't news.'

'Do you really think you can win in the end?'

'Possibly,' he said. 'Just possibly.'

She sat up suddenly, flagpole straight; she said in a voice he had never heard: 'If the Presence weren't with us?'

'What can you mean?'

'If the Presence weren't with us you'd be very much safer.'

'Woman, I do not understand you.'

She sighed and rose. So he wouldn't tell her. He was cooking or had cooked some folly.

The Kashmiri's death had been splashed in headlines and Manerji read his newspapers carefully. There hadn't been the least suggestion that the matter was not what it seemed to be, a particularly brutal hit and run, but Manerji was sceptical and he instinctively discounted coincidence.... So his plan and the Kashmiri's had leaked, he didn't know how but somehow it had. Then the Word had gone out and the Kashmiri had died by it.

Manerji sent for tea and sipped it. It might be his own turn next but he doubted it. If the Presence had wished to end his life it could have done so at any time it pleased for six years at least and probably more, but killing him wouldn't achieve the Presence's end. His property would still pass lawfully to heirs who would pick up the reins and use them. The Presence and the cabal around it had gnawed at the edges and done much damage but he was still an immensely rich man and powerful, powerful in a different way, a way the Presence bitterly hated. And power in a dictatorship was something which could never be shared. Whatever its form there could be only one source of it, and Manerji still had a great deal of say-so. His financial empire had taken knocks but it existed still and still ran pitilessly.

But it might not do that for very much longer—his wife had been right as she often was. The pressure was going on increasingly and that Bill would pass since he couldn't prevent it. The Presence's machine would ram it through. Parliament was a rubber stamp, the most obedient male voice choir in the world. In any conflict under local rules Manerji wouldn't be even a starter.

But he had never intended a fight under local rules. His affairs were international and he had international contacts in plenty. That American had been by far the most potent, and Manerji's plan had been splendidly simple: he'd intended to sell him half of his empire. They'd think twice before they stripped an American when most of the Aid which kept them eating was doled out by the United States.

An excellent idea, but with a snag. For the American hadn't kept his appointment. At first Manerji hadn't been seriously worried, he'd thought he was playing hard to get, but then there had been that polite little note. The American must consult his colleagues, and if and when they reached a decision the American would write again.

Manerji knew what that meant precisely. The banker had changed his mind; he wouldn't deal.

Manerji looked at three clocks on the office wall. One gave the local time in New Delhi, one that of London, the third of New York. The American went to his office early and he could reach him in maybe a couple of hours. He knew his lines were tapped but he'd have to risk it.

Two hours later he received the bad news. Mr. Wallace Noorlander was not in New York. He'd gone to London for a week of meetings, staying at Brown's Hotel as he always did. But it would be better to ring the London office, the London branch of the Noorlander Bank.

Manerji put the receiver down, torn two ways as to what to do. A deal with Noorlander was urgently necessary and Noorlander was New England Dutch. That meant his money was very old money, as old as Manerji's and maybe older. Old money talked the same language everywhere.

Manerji and Wallace Noorlander were men of different colours and backgrounds but they had one thing in common and that an important one. In a world which was trying to rob them both in the name of an unproven philosophy both would fight to the death to hold what they had. Manerji thought his chances were good provided he could get to Noorlander. In time, and that was running out.

But Noorlander was in England—that was bad. Manerji didn't fear the English police; he had decided that they knew the truth, but they wouldn't be there at Heathrow to arrest him any more than the Indian police dared arrest him. The latter were inhibited by the fear of an international scandal, or more accurately they'd been given orders to avoid an international scandal. The English police would be similarly hamstrung. That old hat about a worthless Commonwealth—it kept many officials in pointless jobs. Now if he'd been a Uruguayan. . . .

So the English police wouldn't act but Fenwick might. Three deaths, the Marwadi thought, all men on his ladder. If Fenwick could arrange three deaths he could certainly arrange a fourth. Did he know Manerji's name? Unproven. But it was wiser to assume he did, in which case he'd have a contact in India. Then Manerji couldn't leave New Delhi without his movements being reported to Fenwick.

Manerji shook his head unhappily. In business he was bold and resolute, but in matters of his personal safety, even of his personal comfort, prudence came first by many lengths. He was a Marwadi with that race's great gifts. Cunning was his weapon, not courage.

2

Charles Russell returned to London on an airline with somewhat different mores. Instead of the ritual accepted as real there was an interminable froth of brisk activity. The food was copious but poorly cooked, and was served with a scrupulous care for hygiene which Russell, a cleanly man by habit, considered was overplayed to absurdity. There was telly, and though you needn't listen since the sound came in individual earphones, the flickering box was inescapably present. They were showing an American spy thriller, so far from the world which Charles Russell had known that it left him half way between disbelief and an emotion which was close to anger. When the film was over they dimmed the lights, but Russell couldn't sleep or relax, and in the morning, when he wanted to shave, the tap on one of the basins had broken.

He climbed from the aircraft tired and frayed and took a taxi to his flat to bathe and shave. The bath took the edge from his nervous tension and he decided that he'd lose the rest by going to his club for lunch.

The first man he saw there was Ivan Pendell, and Russell gave him a speculative stare. Sen's death had been in the English newspapers and the proceedings against the north London Irishmen, perfectly fair and proper reporting, but it wasn't being handled sensationally and there wasn't even a whiff of a drug scandal. Russell decided that Pendell looked smug. Well, he had excellent reason to be so. Charles Russell hadn't read Manerji's thoughts but the smother which the Man had expected had in fact been very efficiently organized. Charles Russell wasn't at all surprised. Pendell and the others like him could do this very well when they wanted to.

He walked up to the bar to buy a drink. It was crowded and the only gap was one between Ivan Pendell and the wall. Russell hesitated but finally filled it. He was a courteous man and his conscience was troubled, for he'd been really extremely rude to Pendell. It was true that in St. Agatha's Nursing Home the ass had earned an emphatic brush-off, but if Russell hadn't been in pain, still half-doped on top of the nagging spasms, he'd have chosen a much more civilized phrase to indicate to Ivan Pendell that his presence was no longer desired. There was only way to offer regrets and that was to do so without reserve. He said to Pendell:

'I owe you an apology. May I offer you a propitiatory drink?'

Ivan Pendell turned fishy eyes on Russell. 'I'm sorry,' he said. 'I've a guest for luncheon.' He picked up his drink and walked away. Russell noticed that he sat down alone.

He shrugged; he was neither annoyed nor affronted. He had done what he thought was proper and seemly and if Pendell chose to behave like a boor that couldn't be laid at Charles Russell's door. He smiled as he ordered a second sherry. After all, he'd just saved the price of another.

He finished his leisurely lunch and went back to his flat. There he dozed for an hour, then read Venkata's file, the copy file he'd been given on Manerji. If Russell had ever had doubts that file resolved them. If wickedness had objective meaning here was an unchallenged example. This man didn't need money from drugs, he had plenty, and he'd made it in a way which Russell loathed. Usury. The old words were best. Usury down to the level of villages, the grinding burden on helpless ryots. There were several recent laws against that and more than one from the time of the British, but a man like this one could laugh at the lawbooks. All that was at several removes no doubt—he lent to those who lent again—but the web of his clan was a weed in the soil. At its centre he sat and sucked blood, the blood of countless men in his factories, inefficient and weak because underfed but driven by his professional bullies, the Sikh foremen you found in every mill. Venkata had explained to Russell that the Presence wished to destroy this man. Charles Russell didn't admire the Presence but in that object he was happy to serve it.

And there was something else which the file had told him, something he hadn't known which clinched it. That Sindhi Inspector was in this too, and to Russell that was unforgivable. He had a low opinion of diplomats generally, and diplomats who misused their privileges forfeited all consideration. He had a clear idea of Venkata's plan, which was playing it very dirty indeed, but that didn't lie on Russell's conscience. Now now, not after that shocking file.

Russell put the file in his safe. So far his day had not been agreeable but the evening should atone for it generously. For he'd cabled Penny and Lesley King to meet him for a working supper. William Fenwick was in Northern Ireland.

He was proud of his little serve-yourself suppers and his housekeeper enjoyed them too. Russell opened two bottles of claret and, after hesitation, a vintage port. He seldom drank port wine himself, but King might enjoy it and he was an excellent host.

He was half way through decanting the claret when the doorbell rang. His housekeeper was busy cooking so he put the bottle down and went himself.

It was Shinday in English clothes, expensive ones. Russell said: 'Please come in, Mr. Shinday.' He was a man of sensibility, and to call this dapper figure 'Colour' would clearly be out of place, a clanger.

Shinday came in and sat down when invited to. 'I have to go back tonight so I'll be quick. Manerji is coming to England, though we rather suspect he doesn't want to.' Shinday allowed a smile but left it at that. His English had improved with practice. 'But the Presence is piling the pressure on hard so he's coming to see Mr. Wallace Noorlander. And leaving the same evening.' He named the flights.

'You're sure of all this?'

'He's not tried to conceal it. He knows he can't move without our learning it.'

'And the Noorlander bit?'

'It must have been very urgent indeed. He used his phone for that and he knows we've tapped it.'

Russell nodded. 'Very competent set-up.'

'I thank you sir.'

'Then there's only one thing I need.'

'Quite so. The essential of the whole affair.' Shinday felt

in a trouser pocket, then pulled out a washleather bag. He opened it, displaying the contents. It was no bigger than a Vesta matchbox, say three inches by one and a half. When the lamplight caught it it glittered wickedly.

'You are thinking that it isn't much? But it's the sort that smugglers carry in bodybelts.'

'Just one?' Russell asked.

'Just one is plenty.'

'So Mr Venkata told me.'

'He was right.'

It wasn't for Russell to argue or cavil. Indians knew their own country best. 'Then a happy journey home and my thanks.'

'An honour,' Shinday said.

They shook hands.

When Shinday had gone, Russell turned on the telly. He seldom watched it for entertainment but he liked to look at the evening news. There were the usual disasters of government by Trade Unions and the weather forecast was very bad. A depression over the eastern Atlantic. . . . Toss of superlatively well-kept head of hair. . . . Then thundery showers in south-east of England, winds increasing to gale force rather later. The bland voice droned on and Russell turned it off.

Penny and Lesley King arrived and Russell gave them pre-supper drinks. Later they helped themselves from the sideboard. It wasn't until they had eaten that he gave his news. He hated to mix good food and business.

Penny asked the first question promptly. 'Do we tell father all this?'

Russell rubbed his chin and looked at her sideways. 'What do you think?'

'I was asking you.'

'Your father has uncontemporary values. He's perfectly happy to have a man killed but he's uneasy when a man is framed. You remember those Sikhs? King was going to plant on them. Your father didn't forbid it but he hated the idea of a fiddle. When those Chinese shot the Sikhs he was pleased. He was also, I rather think, relieved. A killing wouldn't strike him as wicked but I strongly suspect that a frame-up would.'

'And what your Venkata now suggests is a set-up?'

'The set-up of all time. An absolute classic.'

'Then we don't tell Father,' she said with decision; she reflected, then asked: 'Do you think it would work?'

'At the Indian end? I'm sure it would.'

'Eight years and probable death for smuggling?'

'That sort's considered anti-social.'

'And what does that mean?' Penny asked at once. She was practical and mistrusted clichés.

'It means whatever you want it to mean in different places at different times. In this country at this unhappy moment it means taking a hard look at realities.' He repeated in rather different words what Venkata had said to him. 'But in India it means what the Presence dislikes. Who's a socialist of a peculiar kind with a taste for fiscal legislation.'

'So Manerji would get the works?'

'You can take it he would if Venkata says so.' He switched from Penny to Lesley King. 'And this end? Could you handle this end?'

King turned to Penny. 'You work at Heathrow. What's pilfering like?'

'Pilfering's a public scandal. There's security of a sort of course, but there's also an efficient Trade Union.'

'That's good,' he said at length.

'But why?'

'If it's easy to whip something out, it's as easy to whip something in. Which is what Venkata is now suggesting.'

'You put it very neatly.'

'Thanks.'

'You could do it yourself?'

'With a bit of practice. It's lucky we still have a little time. This sort of job needs a little time. Rush it and it always falls down.'

'You'll need a Union card,' she said.

'That I can arrange. I have friends.'

'Forgers?' she asked. She hadn't intended to.

King said with a hint of disapproval: 'A very ugly word in the circumstances—I'd rather call them compassionate helpers. There's something called the closed shop, you know, and it often operates pretty maliciously. A man deprived of his job must eat and he probably has only one trade. So he goes to one of my friends who helps him. New name, a new card and of course a new town. I assure you it's disagreeably common.'

Russell repeated: 'A bit of practice?'

'Certainly. So the sooner I start at Heathrow the better. Is it difficult to get taken on?' He was talking to Penny Maxim again.

'I don't know that.'

'Perhaps you don't need to. I've a friend there and perhaps he'll help. More precisely he's going to have to help.'

She said with a touch of her father's asperity: 'You do have some peculiar friends.'

'If I hadn't I wouldn't have lasted a week.'

The party was over; he looked at Penny. 'May I drive you home—it's not out of my way.'

'No need to, thank you, I'm staying the night.'

When King had gone Penny picked up the gold, sliding it on her palm and weighing it. The lamplight caught it again and then moved on. In Penny's hand it looked bleakly sinister.

'It seems a very small thing to break a man's life.'

'You don't need a very thick rope to hang a man. Not in India, that is. Not today.'

3

Manerji had had his hand forced. He had known that the Presence could ram its Bill through, but it wouldn't be the Presence's form to do so without preparing the way. Public opinion was a long way from paramount but it was helpful to have it behind you if you could.

And public opinion was being prepared. There'd been a syndicated article about conditions in one of Manerji's factories, and the tax men had arrived to vet his books. This had happened before and the Man had fixed it: this time he very much doubted he could. The profits he hadn't declared were well hidden, but this time the visitation was serious, not the routine audit he had often bought off. They'd find the two lakhs he had hidden in one place, perhaps even the crore he'd stashed away in another. And there'd been that man on the telly talking nonsense. He hadn't mentioned Manerji's name, but he had said that it was intolerable in this day and age that a tycoon should still have the power he did, the power to decide whether other men ate, the level of employment in cities. It had been routine stuff but ominously timed, and Manerji could read the omens. The heat was really on him now.

Noorlander, he thought—Mr Wallace Noorlander. He had written to say he was consulting his colleagues and Manerji had taken this as the brush-off it very probably was. But he'd have to get to Noorlander somehow. Without American teeth behind him his own empire would fall when the Presence blew on it. But Noorlander was now in London.

As were Fenwick and Russell and Russell's friends.

The Man shivered but he made up his mind. It was a risk but he was obliged to accept it. Money talked louder than physical fear.

He telephoned London, to the Noorlander Bank, making an appointment on Thursday at ten o'clock in the morning precisely. There was a flight which arrived in the early morning and another which left the same evening at seven.

It was useless to try to conceal his movements. He told a secretary to book him openly.

But there was one thing he could do as insurance: he could make that booze-soaked Inspector help him. God knew he had taken money enough, now he could do something to be useful. He had taken to the bottle extravagantly but he was still, till they sacked him, a senior diplomat and had ten days of his tour in London still to run. He'd have the perquisites of his profession, the use of official cars—protection. It was time he did something to earn his money, the money which he'd extorted from Manerji.

Manerji looked at the clock showing London time. The Inspector would have had his lunch and be sleeping it off in a drunken stupor. It would be useless to ring him, he wouldn't be sensible.

The Man sent him a cable with a good deal of malice. He would be arriving in London next Thursday morning, and since the circumstances were exceptional he expected somewhat exceptional treatment. He gave the flight number and the ETA and he looked forward to being met in person. (He nearly added, but decided not to, that the Sindhi must keep sober to do so.) The full treatment, VIP clearance—everything. He would be travelling in comfortable clothes since he hated passing a night in trousers, but he'd be bringing a suitcase with clothes for London and with this they would proceed to the other's flat. There Manerji would change and go on to Cornhill. A High Commission car, of course. After that he would return to the flat where he expected a meal of Indian food and a bed where he could rest for the afternoon. In the evening back to Heathrow again, and again the Inspector would bear him company.

It was a very expensive cable indeed but Manerji didn't begrudge the cost. That Sindhi had made his cut too easily, just keeping his mouth shut and raking it in. It was time he did something positive for it.

In the evening, when his wife came to call on him, he said

to her:

'I'm going to London.' His voice was as cool as it always was but she knew him too well to miss his tension.

'Why are you going to London, then?'

'I have to see a man called Noorlander.'

'Who's Mr. Noorlander?'

'An American banker.'

It's as bad as that, she thought. But she didn't speak.

She went back to her quarters and thought a while, then she sent for her confidential clerk. Her own money was also Manerji's but she still had some which they couldn't touch. A lawyer had told her that already. She and her clerk worked it out together, and she looked at the final figure reflectively. It was enough for her to live on comfortably, even to bring up her children decently. She knew the Presence would strip Manerji bare, it might even contrive to send him to prison. She wondered how she would live as a widow. Not she decided, so very differently. In any normal sense she was one already. She realized she hadn't given him pleasure, but then he hadn't earned much pleasure.

She said to her clerk: 'Sell the lot. Buy gold.'

'Gold here is very expensive indeed. With inflation at the rate it's running—'

'That's why it keeps its value.'

'True. But it's also illegal to hold it in quantity. I don't say bullion can't be found at a price, but there's another risk and that's imprisonment.'

'I pay you very well to serve me. At your age you'd hardly find other employment.'

The Inspector had a doctor in London whom he visited whenever he went there. He had what was called a fashionable practice. He was very expensive but an excellent doctor, and he had, as he needed to have, good judgement of men. He knew when to muffle the drum and when to bang it. This Sindhi was a case for banging it hard. The doctor said simply:

'You're much worse than when you were last in London.'

'In what way am I worse?' The Inspector was resentful.

'I wouldn't care to speak for your liver, your blood pressure is up again, and your heart is under increasing strain.'

'Then what are you going to do for me?'

'Nothing. The only practical thing I can do for you is to send you where you refused to go.'

'I can't do that, I haven't the time.'

The doctor knew that this was a lie. In the morning this man went to his office but seldom before ten o'clock. Then he went home to lunch and got drunk. In the afternoon he slept it off, and then went back to his office to sign his letters. Drunk again in the evening swinishly. There were Europeans who could survive such a life, at any rate for a year or two, but Orientals who took to the bottle hard invariably lasted much less than that. It was interesting, the doctor reflected. There were drugs they could take with apparent immunity, drugs which would soon kill a European, but the moment they switched from what they were used to to alcohol in any quantity you could number their days on a single year's calendar. More from curiosity than a desire for accurate clinical knowledge the doctor asked: 'What do you drink?'

'I mostly drink brandy.'

'I didn't mean which, I meant how much.'

'About a bottle a day.'

The doctor was silent. He had several other patients like this one and the experience to judge quantities accurately. A bottle and a half, he thought — that was the least and maybe two. In any case he was bored with this man and he started to ease him out on a formula.

'Are you sleeping all right?'

'No, not too well, but I take something for it.'

The doctor said sharply: 'I don't remember giving you anything.'

'Oh, it's harmless. You can buy it at chemists.'

The doctor didn't like this news. He guessed that this Indian lied from habit and training, and diplomats had resources which other men had not. He didn't like the Inspector, but the man was his patient. He said on a note of real concern:

'I beg you to be careful, sir. Mix barbiturates with a gutful of brandy and neither I nor anyone else can answer for what could happen thereafter.'

The Inspector went home to a modest drink, modest because the doctor had frightened him. He must cut it down, he really must; he had tried before and failed but he'd try again.

He sat down with his brandy to read his mail. On the top of it was Manerji's cable, and he read it at first without much interest. The Man was becoming by far too demanding, asking to be met in person and treated as a VIP. It was more than his position rated and more than the money he paid the Sindhi could reasonably be supposed to buy. Nevertheless, the Inspector would have to comply. If he didn't the Man could turn awkward and spiteful, and he had more than one way of harming an enemy.

As he put the cable aside the appalling thought struck him down from nowhere. He reached for the bottle again by reflex.

Appalling, shattering, utterly fatal. *Manerji would be carrying drugs.* He had lost three men and that was serious, sufficient warning to any normal man. But Manerji wasn't a normal man, he was a Marwadi and uncontrollably greedy. He was going to bring the stuff over himself and he wanted the Inspector as protection and cover.

He poured a third brandy and hoped it would steady him. It did the reverse since he saw the picture more vividly—the Man coming into the VIP clearance, two briefcases, one in either hand, he himself watching in frozen terror. Then the Customs Officer, cool and polite.

'Your baggage has been cleared already, sir, but perhaps

I could have a glance at your cases.'

And the Inspector would be standing there, all ready to receive a drugrunner. An official car outside. All fixed.

All fixed, but of course he'd deny all knowledge. . . . He could deny in words and deny in writing but he didn't think he'd survive for long. There wouldn't be independent proof whatever Manerji chose to say, but he couldn't walk away from that one. He'd be discreetly recalled to India and he wouldn't find another job there. The Presence would see to that in person.

He looked at the bottle and saw that he'd emptied it. He went to a cupboard and fetched another.

Not go, then? But that could be even worse. If Manerji got through alone he'd be a very angry Man indeed. He'd take a taxi to this flat with his heroin and there he would make even higher demands. He would say that no man could turn his back, no man could just ignore the past . . . 'No, I'm much afraid you're committed, and since you don't comply with reasonable instructions, I'm afraid you may find the next less reasonable. I had plans to replace the late Mr. Sen, but in the circumstances I shall set them aside.' A nod at the two cases on the floor. 'You will take up Mr. Sen's duties while you are here. There is the heroin. See it's distributed.'

The Sindhi took the second bottle to bed with him. He couldn't sleep and he took a tablet. They were what the doctor had feared they might be, for he had bought them at a Cypriot chemist where you could get most things under the counter at a price. For an hour or so he dozed, then woke again. He took another drink, two more tablets.

His servant found him next morning in bed. Manerji had written with malice but he hadn't intended to kill.

He had. Without thinking of justice, he'd seen it done.

4

Manerji had been wrong about Noorlander. He hadn't been playing hard to get, nor had he needed to talk to his board. He'd dropped Manerji like a cigarette end because in Delhi he'd heard repeated rumours. Mr. Manerji was deep in the drug traffic.

It had shaken his stiff New England conscience—one couldn't rub shoulders with men in the drug racket—but as a banker he'd been disappointed. There was business to be done in India provided you watched your step very carefully. There was a bottomless pool of cheap unskilled labour, and unskilled labour under proper direction could be taught to produce a great deal of profit. Tool it up and put in competent managers. Look at the Japanese. He'd been tempted. Of course there were political risks, the Presence the chief of those risks by a mile, but there were risks in every country nowadays and he had contacts in the State Department. They hadn't been precise or definite, no official was ever either by instinct, but they'd shown him the figures for Aid, the real ones. If he bought himself into Indian industry they had doubted if even a power-crazed Presence would do much to put that Aid at serious risk.

So Manerji had been an interesting prospect, and by now, here in London, the banker's private conscience had cooled—the habits of hardnosed business bit deep. He didn't use drugs himself, nor did his family. Drop-outs used them and drop-outs offended him, they flew directly against his ethos and training. But if they didn't get drugs from Manerji they'd get them from somewhere else for certain. In his heart he knew this was rationalization but he was a banker and very rich indeed.

And the Man had forced an appointment on him, one at ten o'clock on Thursday. Very well, he would see him; he'd play it by ear. Meanwhile he intended to lunch at his London club.

He meant to cross Piccadilly the safe way, so he went

down the steps to the Underground concourse. A man was leaning against the wall at the entrance by the sign which said *Gentlemen*. He was surprisingly old for his obvious trade but he gave Noorlander his secret small smile. Noorlander said: 'No thank you,' politely and walked on into the squalid circle.

A girl walked up quickly and stopped in front of him.

. . . Twice in one morning.

Wallace Noorlander was wrong. He saw that the girl was weeping hysterically. 'You've got to help me,' she said. 'You've simply got to.'

He looked at her and his stomach turned over. She'd been pretty once; she was now a wreck. Moreover he could see she was pregnant. 'Just one,' she said. 'Just one fix. I'm desperate.'

Money, he thought. No, that was useless. They always had money, stolen or otherwise. What she wanted he couldn't give her: he had none.

She saw his expression but promptly misread it. 'You've got it, I know. I can always tell others.'

'Madam, I'm sorry. I'm not another.'

'But I know you are. You're just being mean.'

'I'm sorry,' he said again.

She kicked at him. He dodged it and turned on his heel to the stairway. He no longer wanted to lunch at his club, or, for that matter, elsewhere. He felt sick and shaky, spent and miserable. He couldn't have eaten a meal to save his life.

He went up the stairs past the man with the smile and started to walk home, found he couldn't. He leant against a bus stop's pillar till a taxi came by and picked him up.

Back at Brown's hotel he was sick. He lay down for half an hour to rest, then he performed the practised trick which his profession had made a part of his life. He simply wiped his mind quite clean. It was a necessary discipline for any tycoon since without it he'd have been dead in a year — too many accusing ghosts to haunt him, too much distress for a conscience to bear.

He simply expunged the Man completely. Manerji had ceased to exist.

Manerji had been much put out when he found there was no one to meet him at Heathrow. He had expected some smooth young man to contact him, then conduct him through the VIP channel where the Inspector would be waiting obediently with an official car to take them to his flat. When there was none of this the Man was annoyed, but he decided that he would deal with it later. For the moment there were two awkward problems. He recovered his bag but didn't check it through Customs. Instead he sat down to consider the problems which the Inspector's absence had unexpectedly raised for him.

The first was simply a matter of clothing. He had travelled as he'd said he would, comfortably, which meant that he was wearing a dhoti, but he had London clothes in the bag he'd collected and he'd intended to change at the flat at leisure. He didn't fancy a change in a Heathrow lavatory, but he remembered the man in a kilt in New York; what an ass he had looked, how he himself had frowned and blushed for him. Perhaps he could go to an airport hotel, but he didn't much fancy doing that either.

For that brought up the second difficulty, the more serious matter of the solid protection which Manerji would not now receive. He was reasonably sure that the British police had either no desire to molest him or more likely had been ordered not to. But William Fenwick and Russell were not the police. Three men on Manerji's ladder had died. Hotels were out. Even a day alone in London was a risk which perhaps he shouldn't have taken, and if he'd known that the Sindhi would let him down he wouldn't have accepted that risk. For a moment he thought of returning at once. There was a flight at a quarter to ten by a different line, and travelling first class as he was he could probably find a seat on it somehow.

But finally he shook his head. He was here in London for good or ill and his need of Noorlander hadn't diminished. He might conceivably find another protector, but he didn't have any time to play with.

He picked up his bag and went through Customs, the Green Channel since he had nothing dutiable. As it happened he was stopped and examined (perhaps it's the dhoti, he thought) but the search was perfunctory, and the final smile friendly. For Manerji was smuggling nothing, not even a packet of cigarettes. He would never in fact have dreamed of doing so, and if the Inspector had known a little more of the business from which he drew his money he wouldn't have died a squalid death. Drugmasters never carried themselves. That was a rule of the trade and inviolable.

Manerji found a prowling taxi, knowing that he'd be overcharged grossly but anxious to reach Cornhill and safety. He expected to pass most of the day there, and his enemies could hardly touch him in an American bank in the City of London. He looked at his watch: it was a quarter to nine. Much too early for his appointment at ten, but by the time his taxi reached the City somebody should be there at the bank.

Somebody was there indeed for Noorlander's staff arrived at nine. They passed him from doorman to clerk to receptionist, finally to Noorlander's secretary. It wasn't a very comfortable passage since he was conscious of curious eyes on his dhoti. If they'd known it, it was tied immaculately.

Wallace Noorlander's secretary greeted him warmly. She didn't look at his dhoti, she was much above staring, and she put him in the private waiting room.

'I hope you had a good flight, Mr. Manerji.'

'As good as a night flight can ever be.'

'There's a little time to wait till ten. May I offer you some tea?'

'You are kind. But I like it with a lot of sugar.'

'Don't worry, I send a tray. Chinese or Indian?'

'Indian, please. And milk, not lemon.'

When the tea came it was on a silver tray, the crockery unmistakably porcelain. The tea was very good indeed, the best Ceylon, he rather thought.

Wallace Noorlander came in rather late, entering by a door at the back. He hated being saluted by doormen, the curious heads which turned in envy as he walked through the deliberately old-fashioned counting house. He went up in the private lift to his office and his secretary said:

'Mr. Manerji is here.'

'Manerji?' Wallace Noorlander was furious. He'd been able to put Manerji out of his mind and here the man was coming back from the dead. Noorlander said when he'd recovered his temper:

'I do not wish to see Mr Manerji.'

'You agreed to an appointment, sir. He's come a very long way to keep it.'

'Both statements are entirely correct. I simply repeat that I don't want to see him.'

'But if he makes a fuss?'

'Throw him out '

But Manerji wasn't thrown out; he went peacefully.

As he'd done when he'd been driving to London, he looked through the taxi's back window anxiously, but nobody seemed to be behind them. Reassured but by no means wholly at ease he settled to replan his day. He'd be too late to catch that other flight home and his own was not till seven o'clock. That was eight hours, eight hours at risk, so there was only one sensible thing to do. He'd go straight through to the Departure Lounge and there he would sit it out till his flight was called. It wouldn't be too easy to reach him there. If his enemies had made their plans, he had changed his own which would throw them off stride, and to get through to the Departure Lounge there were formalities such as showing passports. Time was short and not every man carried his on him. And thinking of formalities, there were others rather more recent than passports. Security was quietly efficient—all that searching of handbaggage and the machines which showed metal. It would be very hard indeed to conceal a weapon.

Manerji paid his taxi off; he checked in his bag and went through to Departures. Nobody questioned the fact he was early. He bought himself some tasteless sandwiches and a cup of tea which made him wince. He changed it for a glass of water, then settled in a chair to wait. He hadn't slept on the aircraft and by afternoon longed to, but he stayed awake, his eyes moving restlessly. Logic told him he was reasonably safe, but underneath logic he smelt disaster.

Charles Russell answered the clamouring telephone. It was King from Heathrow and he sounded pleased. 'It's all gone well.'

'I'm delighted to hear it.'

'The passengers are still upstairs but the baggage is safely stowed on the plane.'

'*All* the baggage?'

'All the baggage. I go off in an hour and I'll give you details.'

'And I'll give you a very large drink indeed.'

On the aircraft the Man felt safe at last, but though he longed for sleep She withheld her boon. His mind went round and round interminably. He was safe but he had utterly failed . . . Fight the Presence in the courts? Injunctions, appeals to the constitution? The courts weren't yet entirely impotent but such action could only delay, not solve. The weight of metal against him was far too heavy. Given time he might find another Noorlander but time was what he didn't have.

At Delhi he climbed from the aircraft exhausted, walking to the waiting room and watching till his bag came up on the dispenser which worked in fits and starts. A porter tried to take it from him but he could carry it himself and he was mean.

Again he went through the Green Channel confidently and again, as at Heathrow, he was stopped. But this time the manner wasn't friendly. The Customs man was grim and sombre. He made a gesture at his bench.

'On there, please.'

Manerji hoisted his bag.

'Now open it.'

He used his key and opened the lid. For a second he didn't believe what he saw. He didn't speak for some time, he didn't dare to. He said at last, sounding feeble and knowing it:

'That gold isn't mine. I know nothing about it.'

The Customs man stayed in a bitter silence. Two policemen had appeared from nowhere and one of them, Manerji saw, was an officer.

'Mr. Manerji?'

'My name is Manerji.'

'You are under arrest.'

'But Officer. . . .' It tailed away helplessly.

The policeman pointed at the case on the bench. 'You are denying that that is your baggage?'

'No.' It was useless to do so, they could easily prove it.

The other policeman had come forward quietly and Manerji froze in helpless horror. They were going to put the handcuffs on him. . . . He, Manerji, the Man. . . .

He said weakly: 'No. Not that. I beg you.'

'Hold out your hands.' No 'Please'.

He held them out.

The second policeman did it neatly. There were a couple of clicks, then total silence. The steel was cool on Manerji's flesh.

He began to weep softly; then louder, then childishly.

5

Venkata had been to the airport to see Charles Russell back to London. He was going to miss his company and he returned to his office depressed and glum. Surprisingly there was a strange car outside it and a young man he didn't know sat at the wheel. As Venkata came up he got down.

'Mr. Venkata, I think?'

'I am.'

'I'm a friend of your admirer, Charles Russell.'

Venkata was flattered but said: 'I don't deserve his admiration.'

'The Colonel emphatically feels you do.' The man moved to the boot of the car and opened it. Inside were three familiar-shaped cases, the cardboard carefully covered in sacking. 'This isn't in the book of rules but you can't live for ever by reading the book. The labels underneath are a give-away and in my job one has to be reasonably careful.' He looked at Venkata, then added briskly: 'That's three dozen whisky, the best Black Label. Shall I call the porter to take them up?'

'Porters are a curious race. I'd rather take them myself.'

'Then I'll give you a hand, they're surprisingly heavy.'

They took the cases upstairs between them. Venkata said: 'This is much too kind.'

'Colonel Russell doesn't think so, sir.'

'May I offer a drink, then?'

'I'll join you with pleasure.'

When the young man had finished his drink he rose. 'I hope we shall meet again.'

'So do I.'

When he left him Venkata poured a second. He could afford a second drink with three dozen, and probably a third or fourth. As well be hung for a sheep as a lamb.

It was the first English proverb he'd ever learnt and he d learnt it at the Police Cadet School where they'd been teaching him to speak English properly. That was a very long time ago but the life between had not been useless. He had never declined what he saw as a duty and now he had worked with Charles Russell twice, the second time as admitted equal. Who had thought that he rated three dozen whisky.

The tears ran down his fat black cheeks, but he didn't bother to wipe them away. They were the tears of an utter, complete contentment.

Sir William Fenwick had returned from Ulster and Charles Russell had been lunching at Wimbledon. Russell thought Fenwick looked much more relaxed and Fenwick, over brandy, confirmed it.

'You remember my shooting gallery?'

'Yes I do.' The words were spoken with an evident caution—Russell didn't want a repeat performance of an incident which had grated his nerves.

'I've had it dismantled.'

'I think that's sensible.'

'I'm sure it is, and accept my apologies. I'm afraid all that was a bit of a bore.'

'Forget it.' A pause. 'You're looking well.'

'I'm *feeling* well, I have very good reason to. Manerji is in jail and won't come out, and I've another and much more personal reason.'

'Have you indeed.'

Fenwick didn't go on.

'You're being very mysterious.'

'Yes.'

'When am I going to know this great secret?'

'You're, er, dining with Penny tonight, are you not?'

'That's going to be my good fortune.'

'Just so.'

As Russell walked down the drive he turned his head. Fenwick was still at the door politely. Less politely he was laughing happily.

She told him as they woke next morning. 'Charles?'
'Still here.'
'You had lunch with Father yesterday, didn't you?'
'I thought he was looking a whole lot better.'
'He is—he's achieved his real ambition.'
'Putting away that deplorable Manerji?'
'No. He's going to Found his Family after all.'
'You mean he's going to marry again?'
She laughed at him. 'The idea's abhorrent.'
'Take a mistress and acknowledge her child?'
'That would keep it in the family, certainly, but he's got a better way of doing that.'

The coin took a second or two to drop and there were another ten while Russell collected himself. When he'd done so he said in his normal voice:

'But you can't adopt a grandchild, you know. I'm not at all sure that it's even legal.'

'Who's talking about adoption, Charles? When he's old enough he'll take father's name. Daddy will be dead by then but he'll go to his grave a contented man.'

'Suppose it's a girl.'
'It's a boy for sure.'
'You sound very confident.'
'Yes I am. Go and get me some tea before I hit you.'

Russell took his time in making it. The scenario struck him as High Restoration and he hadn't any objection to that, but there was something which wasn't quite right; he must raise it.

'You cheated,' he told her.

'Oh, don't be stuffy.' She giggled, not coyly but in feline amusement, 'You never asked me any embarrassing questions and anyway I always wanted one.'

'I'm glad to have been of service,' he said. The words were formal, the manner wasn't. His moment of doubt had gone with the wind. 'You acknowledge the service?'

'It's acknowledged with love.'

'Any service demands a small fee,' he said.

'I'll pay it with very great pleasure indeed.'

Manerji's wife was with her clerk again. She'd read the newspapers and had formed her opinion but it was sensible to ask a man's too.

'It was a fix, I suppose,' she said.

'It must have been. Manerji would never have chanced it. The risk was far too great for the profit. And it would have been playing into the Presence's hands.'

'Gold,' she said reflectively. 'Gold.'

'Gold was a shrewd choice,' he said.

'And talking of gold—'

'I obeyed your orders. What you own now is solid gold.'

'Where is it, please?'

'In your brother's village. Buried under his house quite safely.'

For a moment she didn't answer him, then she broke into uncontrollable laughter.